Chapter 1

Driving in, weary from the long journey of a thousand miles from Kansas City, Missouri, I brighten up when I see the sign to Stormy, its tastefully crafted letters and beautiful colors. But realizing quickly, it was unfortunately all a ruse. Stormy had left a bad taste in my mouth when I left years ago, only returning for quick visits here and there. This trip down was not only physically draining, but emotionally draining as well. For the first time ever, I would go back to Mama and Daddy's house, being the sole survivor of the family that once inhabited this house.

Rightly so that this town is called Stormy. It has weathered its share of storms, not just the meteorological ones either. There was something about this town that bade warning to those moving in but disguised itself as a gentle spring rain. Stormy displayed its welcoming pineapples and crickets, it's warm and friendly greetings and its beautiful downtown that was graced by overflowing ferns, potted planters of beautiful summer flowers, American flags hung from poles and darling string lights hung around. What wasn't felt was the constant twisting and turning undertow that only dragged you under once you were established there, grounded, roots intertwined.

It was a Wednesday the day that I arrived and multicolored tents crowded the square grounds with local farmers, artisans and small business owners gaining favor with those who bought their produce and wares on a weekly basis with a few curious visitors sprinkled in the weekly mix.

This particular day that I came back to take care of family business was oppressive, a ubiquitous cloud forcing its presence on an already worn-out soul. It was the last of the liquidation of the meager estate of my parents. The remnants of their entire lives wrapped up in a house that begged for attention. Mama had lost her mind in this town. Literally, had gone deeply into dementia triggered by so much abuse and mind games not only played by her family, but the townspeople as well.

Things did not end well for her. She was not the same person she was when we were growing up. Hallucinations brought her joy and company, but abuse continued until the end. Her story would take volumes to write and that is a project for another day.

My heart hurts that she sacrificed to provide a place of safety in what she thought was a safe town. I guess what you don't know doesn't hurt you right? Or so it seemed.

It was Wednesday evening of my first day there. I opened all the doors to the rooms, turned on the whole house fan and set up my room. Uncovering my four-post canopy bed, I sat down on the side and shed a little tear. Mama had been the last one to make up this bed. She would have stripped the bed as soon as I left, washed the linens and remade the bed in anticipation of the next visit, only I didn't' came back very often to Stormy to visit. We had her moved to Mobile to a more advanced facility than they could provide in Stormy.

I didn't really come back to visit her as often as I wanted until she was nearly gone. She didn't recognize me for who I was, only that I shared DNA with her abuser. Even though I couldn't help that fact, I knew that my visits only agitated her more and I laid low when I did come to visit. I kept daily checks on her and made sure she had her candy bars and cokes. That always made her happy.

I finished putting my things away, turned the water on at the road and then got myself a cup of tea. Everything was how she left it last time she was here. Dust now covered everything. It had been years since she had last stayed here for any length of time.

I changed into my pajamas and sneaked out the back door and down the worn path to Miss Nella's house to let her know I'd made it to town. Her name was Jan Ella, but somewhere down the line I started calling her Miss Nella.

It was warm out, but Miss Nella's patio was equipped with a fan that blew all the time. I sat down on the swing for a minute to just soak it all in. Ferns were placed so nicely on the four corners of the patio, planters and pots of petunias and geraniums were everywhere. "How wonderfully inviting!" I thought. Before I even knocked on the door, Miss Nella came hurrying down her back stairs making giddy noises and wiping her hands on her favorite apron. I sprung to my feet and ran over to hug her "Oh baby girl I thought you weren't going to be here 'til later tonight. I just happened to see you in the security camera when I glanced over at it. I'm so glad you're home now. How long can you stay?" asked Miss Nella with hopeful eyes. "Well, I'm gonna play it by ear, but it may take me most of the summer to get the house ready to sell. Just knowing I've got you next door will make this trip a whole lot easier Miss Nella. Stormy hasn't always been good to me, but I'm hoping to lay low and just get the house ready to sell," I told her. "You and I both know you are not going to lay low. You have a writer's mind and I know your curiosity will lead you on all kinds of adventures this summer. Just be careful Cacky, this town is not what it seems," Miss Nella warned me. "I will, I promise." I gave her a tight hug and told her I was headed back over to the house to get some things in order. "I promise I'll be by in the morning. Goodnight my sweet Miss Nella" I turned to go. "Good night my sweet Cacky. I will expect you for breakfast in the morning but sleep as much as you need. It will be ready when you get here." Miss Nella watched as I walked back down the path to our house.

Thankfully I had switched the back porch light on before going to Miss Nella's. The sun seemed to have lost its grip and sank quickly over the horizon. The frogs were singing and the fire fireflies were making their yearly debut. She was right about my writer's mind. I had already had many things that I was processing as I walked up the stairs of the back porch. The last of the wisteria blooms' fragrant smell garnished my attention for a brief moment, but turning back to prior thoughts of Miss Nella had my mind racing. Why would Miss Nella have an alarm system and cameras? We never even had to keep the doors locked most of the time, much less an alarm system. I guess I've been gone too long. I wasn't spooked or scared or at least I didn't think I was until the front porch light automatically switched on. I about jumped out of my skin until I remembered I had set a timer on that light several years ago. "Good grief! Why was I acting so scared," I muttered out loud. I had protection with me. That was something I never traveled without anymore. Living in Kansas City, it was a necessity. Allowing my mind to settle down, I drifted into a deep sleep that provided the rest I needed to start my adventures in Stormy.

Chapter 2

I heard the courthouse clock chime ring seven and I hopped out of bed. Since I got up much earlier than I thought I would, I phoned Miss Nella to tell her I was going to get doughnuts for us this morning. She let me know she hadn't expected me to be up this early and would welcome a doughnut from Sweet B's Bakery. I got dressed and headed out. After circling the square three times and still not finding a place to park anywhere, I gave up. Halfway around the 4th circling, I turned right to make my way back behind the square to a route through a less busy neighborhood. On my way around, I saw Nola Mae sitting in her side yard curled up in a ball and whimpering. She had to be in her 60s, I remember her being about 10 years older than me, but right now she looked like a small child all curled up. I stopped by to see if she was alright. As I approached her, old man Mr. Blankenship hollered from his porch "You better leave her alone if you know what's good for you! That woman's crazy!" At first, I thought the gesture was a caring warning, but the look on his face was more of a threat to me. "Well, it looked like she had fallen, and it didn't hurt for me to stop and check on her," I replied. He grumbled and mumbled something under his breath. It didn't sound very nice. I had enough of him already. I made my steps more purposeful than before. He wasn't gonna tell me what to do so rudely. When he went inside, she released herself from the curled-up state. Helping her to her feet, I told her I'd be back to check on her. She whimpered, "Thank you."

As I drove on back towards home my mind was going crazy. Mr. Blankenship was always so grumpy and honestly full of himself. He always got under my skin when I worked as a teenager at the accounting firm on the square. I couldn't stand to be around him. He always carried a foreboding spirit.

Only twelve hours into my visit to Stormy and I had already made an enemy. After parking my car in the driveway back at home, I decided it wouldn't hurt me to walk to Sweet B's to get those doughnuts.

It didn't take long to get there by walking and that should have been what I did to start with, I guess. What in the world was going on downtown? There were news cameras set up everywhere and all the shops were open. Their sandwich boards all displayed their daily specials or sales. Goodness, it had really grown. I made my way to the bakery hoping I wouldn't see anyone I knew. But then like a jack-in-the-box, Cil Landry pops up from a patio table near the coffee shop and yells "Cacky!" Pretty sure I deflated some right there in front of her, but she pretended not to notice. She approached me with a kiss-kiss and a light hug. I'm quite certain she didn't want to mess up her fancy new green dress. She said she knew I was coming because her best friend's mother was my realtor. Wish I had just skipped the doughnuts this morning. Who needed Cil Landry to know your business? She said she would be checking in on me as she scooted off to her group at the table who all waved with fake smiles conjured up by Cil's excitement. At first glance they collectively looked like a bowl of summer salad with sweet peas, carrots, radishes and cucumbers. This visual helped me to find humor in this situation and guided my return walk home to the opposite side of the courthouse. It was well worth the extra steps to avoid another conversation with Cil.

The walk home was flooded with so many things I wanted to ask Miss Nella about. I was pretty sure I would overwhelm her with all my questions, so I mustered up some control and dictated into my phone. Recording all my thoughts so I wouldn't forget to ask everything that was top priority this morning. "Poor Miss Nella," I thought as I reached her sidewalk and walked up the front steps.

Chapter 3

About to burst, I rang the doorbell at Miss Nella's. She answered quickly, being notified by her alarm system that someone had approached her front door. I could hear the notification even through the door. I guess you get used to something like that when you live alone.

"Miss Nella, what is going on downtown? Yesterday when I drove into town, it looked like the idyllic small Southern town. Now it looks like a movie set has popped up ready to film on location." I said without taking a breath. "And I couldn't find a place to park anywhere. That is what took me so long. I'm sorry." I said as I handed her the box of doughnuts. "Sit down, Cacky," she gestured toward the swing. "Well, several things had crept into town finishing off the already extremely impoverished and destitute town that Stormy was. We went through a period of time that was absolutely devastating. Many people didn't have jobs, some major storms blew through, including a horribly destructive hurricane. All these elements caused major hardships in this town. Families struggled and many ended up in separation and eventually divorce.

It was once rumored, but then proudly professed by the judge herself, that she encouraged and arranged very speedy divorce proceedings. She was granting divorces without questions, counseling, parenting classes and honestly looking over procedural mistakes as well. Apparently, this particular judge, who still remains judge, had experienced a long, painful divorce herself before moving to Stormy. She had to endure the counseling and parenting classes. She told some mutual friends that she only wished for a speedy one so she could legally marry her longtime boyfriend.

"Good grief, Miss Nella that's horrible. I'm guessing they "lived happily ever after" then?" "Haha no mam. The boyfriend got tired of waiting on the divorce to go through and ended up running off with another woman from North Alabama. Well, this set in motion a grand scheme to create a culture within a small community where family litigation was easy and painless. Though divorce or any other family law is never really painless, she brought her talents to Stormy and used the town as her litigation playground. She quickly gained favor in the eyes of the townspeople as she campaigned for fast and friendly divorces. Many people had been through so much already with the economic downturn. They could only see this as a positive in the town. They had no idea what it would truly result in. But her ideas were very popular and her calculated timing of elections landed her a mighty powerful position at the courthouse. The next years would be instrumental in Stormy's growth in wealth and prosperity, something that hadn't been seen in years. A dredge of the goodness that was left was replaced by evil." Miss Nella concluded.

"It sounds like a drive through service for fast food. Honestly, I am a little numb at the moment. This whole thing is crazy. It is just so unbelievable, though I can see its workings in everything now," I said still shocked at the information.

"Yes, Cacky, the divorce rate here quicky skyrocketed to an increase of 250% the first six months she was judge. Some marriages dissolved after one or two years. It is so sad. News reporters caught wind of what was going on in Stormy and started writing story after story of this takeover of Stormy dubbing it the "Litigation Center of Alabama."

"Attorneys from all over were beginning to flock to the town, some working as a mobile unit or satellite office while others decided the trend was substantial enough to plant themselves here and grow roots in the town. With plenty of attorneys present, the cost was low, the work was lucrative as they handled as many cases as possible. With the guaranteed sign off from the judge, the attorneys could pump out cases without having to worry about scrupulous information gathering or proper procedural checks. It was like the judge stamped approval with her left hand while reading the next case to her right." Miss Nella paused.

"Were there that many people in the Stormy area seeking divorce, Miss Nella? That seems excessive." I commented, puzzled.

"Oh, honey people came from all over Alabama to get a quick and easy divorce. It was like Las Vegas is for weddings, only for divorces. As more visitors came, the need for food, lodging and other necessities became a jackpot of a business opportunity for the locals and they jumped quickly on it with such excitement and zeal. The downtown was completely revamped, and many people turned homes and businesses into places of lodging to supply the overwhelming need."

"So that is why there are so many food trucks and no places to park today. That sure does explain it," I said in a frustrated tone.

"Well not really, at least not anymore. The recognition that the town got in major newspapers across the state brought on the idea that Stormy was the perfect spot for change of venue cases that were high profile. They were welcomed by locals, both attorneys and businesses. And that's where we are now. Thursdays are big days now as cases start on Thursdays here. It was a deal we made with somebody down the line. Stormy residents would attend to their business Monday through Wednesday and Thursdays and Fridays were reserved for change of venue cases. I guess we all got used to it. I had not even thought to warn you about that.

"I'm definitely keeping that in mind while I am here this summer. It will save me many headaches," I said thankfully. "And I might just have to do some walking on the square on Thursdays, just to drink in the details of this change in Stormy. Might be some good material for a book." I laughed. "I don't like the way it came about,

15

but I would like to put the pieces together of this transition of Stormy going from destitute to the "Litigation Center of Alabama". I've got too much to do today unless my curiosity gets the best of me.

"By the way I stopped by Nola Mae's this morning. She was curled up in a ball on her back lawn and I went to check on her. I thought she had fallen. She isn't that much older than me, but we can take a tumble at any age really, so I stopped. Old man Mr. Blankenship came out on the porch and told me to leave her alone in such a mean tone. Miss Nella, I'm ashamed to say I was quite disrespectful to him, but I wasn't standing down. I was only checking on Nola Mae and he acted like I was trespassing. There was something not right about all of it, but I can't put my finger on it. I told her quietly that I would be back. I think I might take her some doughnuts next time."

"You be careful Cacky. Nola Mae is known in town to be crazy. Just be real careful," pleaded Miss Nella. I promised I would.

Chapter 4

Well, my curiosity got the best of me. Today was a busy day downtown. I wanted to see what all the fuss was about when a big change of venue case came to town. I had noticed all the food trucks had already started getting the early spots for quick access of hungry media correspondents and cameramen, people in town for the case and the townspeople who felt like every time a big case came to town, it was like a major festival happening.

I got Maisy all harnessed up to take another morning walk around the square. She was ready for a walk. She and Miss Nella's Maine Coon Cat, Malcolm had been lounging on her porch while we had breakfast and talked about all we had read in the Press Register about the case.

The morning was humid, and I was so glad I had gotten that haircut that I always dread getting. I would have had hair plastered to my neck by now if it was longer. But getting out for a walk, even as humid as it was, is what I needed too. So, we set out on an adventure.

As I walked, my mind began wandering to the reasoning behind the case. This case was based on a woman who had killed her husband when she found out he had been leading a double life. Even though she had enjoyed the spoils of his lucrative business, she hadn't known about his dual life that began with a relationship online.

I got to thinking about how technology, I'm sure, had done a number on Stormy, too. Social media algorithms tagged people for facial recognition, bringing to light affairs of the past. I'm sure people started recognizing how many people looked alike and started asking questions. I wondered how much of this had affected Stormy and if it played any part in so many people getting divorced.

Online DNA tests would have divulged what we call in my family "doughnuts". Since having our social media group for extended family, I have met so many people who are related to me somehow. Some are related multiple ways. When the circle keeps going, we call that a doughnut. Back in the day, having too few people within a small radius forced people to marry whoever was available. Sometimes those people were kin. You married whoever lived within walking distance or a short ride on your beloved horse. My granddaddy said that before there were vehicles to transport you around, there was slim pickins'. I always chuckled a bit when he said stuff like that. As time went on, the familial tree branches reached into neighboring towns and counties, spreading out the DNA.

Then my mind shifted to another element of technology, pornography. What an absolute horror show that was and still is for so many people. Stormy surely got hit hard with this too. Its prevalence in all areas of the country resulted in such addiction and abuse. The marriages that were already weak, were aggravated by this evil addiction. Ultimately even strong marriages crumbled under the weight of its abuse. I bet Stormy didn't escape this one either.

Such heavy thoughts had been circulating in my head and I had not realized that I had already made it to town. Stopping at the bakery to get a cup of water for Maisy, I ordered myself an iced coffee to cool off. I sipped slowly while watching all of the people scurrying around setting up for the day. It is always so entertaining to people watch.

My mind went back to technology that more than likely affected Stormy. New investigative measures and processes eased the burden of solving crimes. Sadness washed over me for a brief moment remembering some of the crimes that had been unsolved before this great enlightenment. It made me hurt for the family members that had been left with years of unanswered questions and no closure. Technology had definitely improved the chances of people being caught, but even with the fanciest of all equipment, technology and processes, humans still played a huge role in deciding who gets blamed and prosecuted. Cover ups, pay offs, hush money and threats still existed almost as they were before technology came to Stormy. Mama told me some of these stories all along.

Shouting across the way jolted me back into the scene in front of me. An older man was yelling really loudly in a panicked voice, extremes of pitch as he barked and roared. Maisy and I decided that we would walk over that way to assess the situation.

When we approached the mayhem, I recognized the man as Mr. Charlie Pugh. It had been years since I had seen him, actually thirty years. Charlie Pugh was what we would call a "wheeler dealer". He didn't blink an eye to make a deal right out from under you and you wouldn't even know what happened. He was a very popular man, very social. He threw the best elite society parties. Anybody that was anybody in Stormy wanted to attend. Honestly, I think people were afraid not to attend. Mr. Pugh's ego was fed by his parties" attendance numbers. I remember babysitting for him a couple of times at his estate as a teenager. He was very self-absorbed and mean spirited to people working for him. That's one of the reasons I only babysat a couple of times for him.

As we continued closer, I could hear the conversation more clearly. Propping myself against a large pin oak tree, I focused intently on the conversation.

Mr. Pugh began shouting directly at his secretary who was fumbling with several sets of keys, apologizing over and over to the people standing behind her, laden with suitcases and equipment. They were all waiting to check in to their respective places of stay.

"Beth what do you mean those keys don't work? They worked a month ago when I had them installed. Did you lose the keys?" He screamed edging towards her angrily. He never used to get quite this angry or at least I never saw him this way.

There were more people coming up the sidewalk ready to check in to Mr. Pugh's newly renovated apartments and rooms overlooking the courthouse and its gardens. He hurriedly walked to the other properties demanding that Beth follow to check those keys too. Beth, losing her breath and her will said defeatedly, "Mr. Pugh none of the keys work." She collapsed onto a nearby bench and began to weep uncontrollably. She put her hand over her face and said "I've tried them all." Charlie Pugh being completely engulfed in a fit of rage, called Sheriff Pete Tucker. "Pete, Charlie Pugh here. You better get down here right now. Something is going on and I demand you take care of it." From the look on Mr. Pugh's face, the Sheriff wasn't giving in to his demands. Charlie violently threw his phone down and started screaming at his secretary again. She cried even harder this time and gathered herself tightly in the corner of the bench.

Sheriff Tucker arrived with all the fanfare of lights, bullhorn for crowd control and the snarkiest grin I had ever seen. He sidled over to Charlie Pugh and began a slow laugh at seeing him in this condition. Charlie's linen suit had completely been soaked by sweat from the stress and the summer heat. It had changed its original wheat color to a darker shade of brown. Sheriff Tucker motioned for his deputy and told him to take Beth back to the office and help her calm down.

Now the real conversation was beginning. Positioning myself behind the tree even closer than before, I felt like I was watching an interrogation behind one of those two-way mirrors.

"Well Charlie, where do I start? Maybe I will start with the fact that your underhanded acquisition of these properties has finally come back to bite you! Your arrogance and greed have caught up with you. You kicked many people out of their businesses and put them out of a job. Didn't you know that all of this would come back on you?" Sheriff Tucker seemed very satisfied in telling Charlie all of this.

Charlie, not fazed at all by listening to his remorse provoking monologue, stared straight into Pete's face, pointed his finger and yelled "What did you do Pete?" "It's what I didn't do, Charlie, that makes this such a satisfying end to your career." The sheriff turned and talked to his deputy. "Preston, tell them it's okay to let them into the apartments." Sheriff Tucker grabbed hold of Charlie as he lunged forward like a wild animal. Pete Tucker held him back and threatened to lock him up. Charlie growled at him, "Why is Welsh Daniels letting these people in? Where did he get keys?"

"Well Charlie, they came with the titles to the properties. It all looked legit to me." The Sheriff said snidely. "Welsh said he won them at a poker game and I believe him. You never were very good at poker." Sheriff Tucker said, "But you were always a good cheater. It looks like you have met your match." Pete Tucker had been waiting years to get at Charlie.

With pure satisfaction the Sheriff left the scene with a stunned Charlie Pugh frozen on the sidewalk. "You know, Pete Tucker, you know you are in an elected position!" Charlie bellowed after the sheriff. "The town doesn't like you as much as they don't like me, Charlie Pugh. And it looks like this time you won't have the capital means to buy it off," retorted Pete. "Old money can't compete with modern technology." Pete watched Charlie slither back down to the ground in defeat. And to add insult to injury, Sheriff Tucker said, "Oh Charlie, one last thing. You stole my whole world all those years ago and now it looks like someone is stealing yours." Charlie looked down at his wedding band. "Like you told me years ago Charlie, when you underhandedly took Tracy from me, "That's too bad, but get over it!"

I gasped at hearing this information. I had no idea all of this was going on. Recently I had heard about title theft but hadn't known anyone that it had happened to. Walking back toward the direction of home, I couldn't wait to tell Miss Nella what had happened. Maisy couldn't keep up with my quick pace, so she gratefully traveled in my arms the rest of the way. Dripping with sweat and out of breath, I reached Miss Nella's front porch.

Chapter 5

Friday downtown was busier than Thursday. Court was in session for another day, and the crowd had doubled. This must have been a bigger case than I thought. Walking was the most efficient and successful way to get downtown now. I went by Sweet B's again this morning to get a couple of doughnuts for Nola Mae. I made the loop and ended up at Nola Mae's.

"Let's go sit a spell," Nola Mae offered. "I just oiled my settee, so it glides mighty nicely." As inviting as her offer was, I had such an eerie and uncomfortable feeling as we walked through her yard. It felt like someone was watching us, probably Mr. Blankenship. Not seeing him anywhere I still couldn't shake the feeling. She obviously felt something too because she abruptly got silent and nibbled on her doughnut like a small child would, nervously.

As many years as I had taught school, I had only seen this kind of behavior in trauma situations of abuse or a child experiencing another kind of traumatic event. It had been like a switch was flipped. This must have been the same behavior she exhibited to the townspeople, along with her stories about the headless woman carrying around a baby. No wonder they thought she was crazy. But I didn't get the crazy part, I got the trauma response from her. The only trigger that I noticed was when Mr. Blankenship came out on his porch the other day. Was he lurking around, and I didn't see him?

Nola Mae was only about ten years older than me. She looked a lot older and certainly dressed older in her floral house dresses she undoubtedly got from her mother's closet and her flip flops. Resting my hand on her shoulder, I gave her a look of understanding and heartfelt care and moved in the direction of the front yard. "I will be back to see you. We've got so much catching up to do." I winked at her and turned back again. Out of the corner of my eye I caught a glimpse of a figure peering through a window and then it vanished. It was Mr. Blankenship, of course.

Mr. Blankenship had always seemed like a coarse man. His daughter was in my class at school. She was always nice, but she left town as soon as she had a chance like so many did. I didn't blame her at all.

Finishing my doughnut, I started walking in the direction of home. Heading back to the house, I was gearing up mentally to pack some more and retouch some of the paint on the walls. But my thoughts kept going back to Nola Mae and I couldn't shake them. Unlocking the door and heading inside I kept going over in my mind what had happened this time and the last. Why was she so triggered by Mr. Blankenship? What had happened?

Nola Mae threaded through my thoughts the rest of the day. I worried, prayed and tried to release that eerie feeling, but just couldn't. If Mama were here, what would she tell me? I know exactly what she would say. She would say "Cacky, I tried to help her, it put me to bed." Now I certainly could understand that.

Mama's empathetic tendencies many times put her to bed. She just about could feel the stress and strain on other people. She felt deeply and I could see her being around Nola Mae could have set her back a week or so. She was very much a physical empath.

Getting distracted looking through old letters that my grandma wrote to my mother was probably the best thing I could have done that day. I loved reading what my grandma wrote, giving such detailed accounts to such mundane activities. She always had a way with words.

I found myself drifting off as I lay on the sofa reading the letters and allowed myself to surrender to sleep. A short nap would be helpful as I found myself emotionally exhausted from the day.

Chapter 6

Porch chats at Miss Nella's with her transplants were very nice. I had made it a mission while I was in town to go and try to join them when they had their porch chats as much as I could. Usually, it was around 4:30 or so on Tuesdays and Fridays. These women had come from all different places in the country and landed here in Stormy by some means. One of their parents had relocated or they had married somebody from here, or their husband's job had transferred them here. However they arrived, they were transplants and seemed to all be affected the same way by Stormy's undercurrent.

Miss Nella's house was a place of safety and a place to voice grievances, concerns or just catch up on the latest Stormy news. I wouldn't say there was gossiping going on. It was what my Mama called whispers on the wind, more of a concern than gossip. So many times, these women had been the subject of hateful gossip in Stormy and Miss Nella's porch chats helped to validate the members even when Stormy society had claimed or procured invalidation for these transplants.

Miss Nella always made sure she had plenty of snacks and tea or coffee and a comfy place to chat during the spring, summer and fall. These chats were held on the porch and each seat was filled by someone needing to be there. In the winter, the chats moved inside, but usually to the sunroom at Miss Nella's. No matter, it was a welcomed reprieve on each occasion. On this particular day, Miss Lolly, who lived three doors down was telling us about something that had happened recently to her side neighbor. She starts in after tasting one of Miss Nella's lemon cookies. "Fuel for my heart, Jan Ella. These are the best lemon cookies I have ever had," said Miss Lolly as she made 'hmm mmm' noises. I wanted to tell y'all that we might have a new member for our porch chats." "Really? Who?" Miss Nella inquired. "Well, you know Sissy, my side neighbor?" "Yes" everyone nodded. Miss Nella reached for her pen and a notecard. That was odd, but I thought maybe she was multi-tasking with a list for groceries or something. She used to always have a pen and notecard on the porch. I always assumed that was what it was for. "Well she is having the hardest time with her husband and that woman he moved in with them." Everyone gasped at Miss Lolly's announcement. "Oh my word!" Miss Nella spoke first. "I had no idea poor Sissy was having to deal with that. She is such a dear! Cacky, you would like her. She is just a bit younger than you and has been a teacher for a long time too. Lolly, please tell her to sit with us when she can," Miss Nella pleaded. "I will first chance I get. Thank you for making a place for her. She needs us right now." Miss Lolly said gratefully.

Everyone filled up on goodies and news. One by one they left the porch to go about their evening duties with their families. All that was left was me and Miss Nella. "Miss Nella, I sure have missed you. I'm sorry I haven't been back. Once Mama passed, you know I moved Daddy up to Kansas City with me. He wasn't doing too good. As mean as he was to Mama and all of us really, I felt it was my obligation to take care of him. He wasn't any nicer than he used to be, but I did what I had to do. I'm sure Mama told you about him. I sure hope she did. I hope you believed her too. It was all true."

Miss Nella sighed, shook her head and looked sweetly toward Heaven. "Your mama is healed now. She is happy and whole." I knew Miss Nella was right.

"Miss Nella what all happened to this town? Wasn't it a good place to live? I know I had my share of problems with Stormy, but I thought maybe it was just me." I sat on the edge of my seat in anticipation.

"Oh Cacky, this town hasn't really changed. It's protective veil has been removed, but it is no different than it was fifty years ago…a hundred years ago. It is just now out in the open. Plain as day and disgraceful as ever. If I hadn't established my garden years ago, planted all my fig trees and crepe myrtles, I probably would not have stayed. Thomas left me plenty and plenty to share so I have just been finding those people who need me. It has satisfied me all these years after his passing. My days are fair to midland and that is enough."

"How come I never knew how bad this town was when I lived here?" I asked. "You didn't need to know. It is quite a burden once you do. Your mama knew you saw enough in your own house to worry you. She hid a lot of what happened in the town. What used to happen in the cover of darkness has now been deliberately brought to light. I think it brought comfort to those who had been carrying the burden of secrecy all those years. Now with the judgment bar set so low, people are free to live how they want and not have to worry. Makes my heart so sad to see it all so public and accepted. I just keep to myself as much as possible, except for my friends that come by for porch chats or just to sit a spell."

"Miss Nella, what kinds of things happened when I lived here? I just don't remember anything that bad. I am old enough to handle it now," I laughed.

"Well sugar, I will be right back." Miss Nella left where she was sitting, walked in the house letting the heavy hinged door slam behind her. I missed that sound. It was always a comfort.

Miss Nella came back and sat down with a recipe box in her hand. I looked at her puzzled and thought maybe she forgot what we had been talking about. "This right here is history, plain and simple. On these cards are the happenings of this town from the time you were a teenager up until this week. Anytime there was something that happened that was important, I wrote it down."

I looked up so surprised and jumped up. "That's why you always had a notecard and pen on the porch." "Yes mam! I kept one in case something important came up in conversation. Then I wrote notes on what had been said." Miss Nella explained.

"What a treasure trove of knowledge you are holding in your hand. You will have to tell me some of the stories that you have written down. I would love to hear them!"

"Well, I can certainly do that! Just you wait!"

Chapter 7

My cousin Ivy Mac had come up from Mobile for a couple of days to help me while I was working on Mama and Daddy's house. She could only spare a couple of days because their business was in a busy season. She did some of the work off site, but most of her work had to be done on site. We made the most of our time together.

Dinner options in Stormy sure had blossomed while I was gone. So much has been put into the service industry since the high-profile trials had made their way to Stormy. Thankful for the options but not sure I like the way it all came about. Nonetheless having several places to choose from, we went to the Camelia Bar and Grill hoping it was more of a grill than bar. Locating at the end of the block was a smart business move with limited parking elsewhere around the square. This was the place to go if you wanted to park the car and go in.

Large ferns graced the entrance, with its grand oak doors that were mighty. Inside was lighted only with individual wall sconces that provided a glow for each booth. Not a bad setting for the ending of a very hard day of packing and cleaning.

The waitress came around and took our orders. I recognized her from school but she was much younger than I was, actually five or six years younger. I didn't bring attention to the fact that I knew her because I wanted to focus on spending time with Ivy Mac.

Glancing around, the food looked delicious. We ordered and continued our ongoing conversation from the day. Ivy Mac filled me in on some of the cases that had come here from Mobile, and we talked about some of the things that Miss Nella had told me. I hovered over the table to get closer and whispered to her about the incident that happened with Mr. Blankenship. It was so unnerving retelling it that when the waitress came back with our food, we both jumped as she greeted us. We giggled a bit and then began to dive into our lovely dinners.

About the third bite in, I had a very foreboding feeling as if someone was watching me. I thought maybe I had just spooked myself talking about Mr. Blankenship. Looking around the restaurant just to reassure myself, I was comforted by seeing mostly business attire. That was quite fitting as there were many people in town for the murder case down from Birmingham going to trial this week. Reassured, I turned my attention back to Ivy Mac. "I know that look Cacky. What did you see?" Ivy Mac said. "I'm sorry. Not a thing, thank goodness!" I said relieved.

We enjoyed another relaxing hour just chatting about everything. Feeling it was time to go, we headed out. We both slid to the end of our sides of the booth, grabbed our purses and straightened out our clothes to exit the restaurant. We thanked the waitress and headed out.

As we passed the bar, a man turned around and glared at me. You know that look when you rub a cat's back fur the wrong way? That was the look he was giving me. Judging by the two bowls stacked on each other and the three empty beer glasses, he had been there a while. I nonchalantly walked past him, ignoring his pointed stare, pulled back my shoulders and went confidently out of the building. Mr. Blankenship wasn't going to determine the mood of my evening.

Confused by my sudden change in behavior, Ivy Mac slipped her arm in mine and followed in lockstep quickly out the door. "What was that all about?" Ivy Mac asked. She turned me to face her. My shoulders collapsed and I told her about my most recent encounter with Mr. Blankenship. "That sorry thing!" Ivy Mac said exasperated. "Ivy Mac, he seems to pop up in many of the places I go and it's becoming rather uncomfortable. I know he's an old man, but Ivy Mac he seems to be a very busy one. Well, whatever, let's enjoy the rest of the evening. The stores on the square open late so let's go peek in a few."

Allowing any fear or awareness to disrupt our evening, we walked up to the first shop. It was a local bookstore and coffee shop. We headed in for a piece of key lime pie and decaf giggling about them having any of my books in their shop. After enjoying our treat, we walked to the back to try to find one of my books. There they were on the shelf, not really in plain sight. Seeing them wedged between other books, we exited the shop. Must have been my punishment for being gone too long and speaking on subjects they just didn't want to hear. This town, with its roots so embedded and intertwined with the past could only grow on the surface. It made me proud of myself for embracing a subject that made the town uncomfortable. We finished up our conversation of triumph and marched on to the next store, Robin's Nest.

The placement of the lights were so darling and Robin had such beautiful taste and a heart of gold to match. Robin was a cousin who I knew would do anything for me or anyone else. She has such a strong spirit and is such a hard worker. I'm so proud of her success and thankful she could find the good in Stormy, even after experiencing the bad.

She wasn't working this particular evening, but I wanted to brag on her and the store. We looked for a bit at the jewelry and décor items then went to take a look at some things in the back of the store. There were soaps, fragrances and kitchenware. So many lovely things to look at. We had only been back there for a few minutes when we heard the lady at the register say "Well hey Mr. Blankenship, what brings you in this evening?" He mumbled something to her that I couldn't hear. I froze in panic. Ivy Mac looked at me and I motioned to her for us to proceed to the stockroom. Ivy Mac gave me a worried look, but quietly moved toward the very back. Floors creaked slightly but we made it all the way to the very back of the building. "Hey, this door goes out to the alley." I pointed. We pushed quietly out the door, assuring that the door didn't slam.

We take off running out of the alley and rounded the corner to the square, only to see Mr. Blankenship standing outside of the store. He was looking to the north and then the south to see if he could find us. "Glad you were here Ivy Mac, this is getting ridiculous. He must be scared out of his wits about something or mad about something. I just figured he was a bored old man, but I do believe there's more to it and I need to find out!" Ivy Mac now gave me a stern look. "You better be careful. I'm not kidding you. We both know what nefarious things happen in this town." Ivy Mac said waving her finger at me. "You know I'll be careful, but you also know I'm not going to be bullied into staying away from someone who I believe needs my help." I said sternly back. "I know you're not and if it was me in the same position, I would do that too." "I know you would Ivy Mac. You of all people understand me. Now let's go

41

home. Maybe we can try again in the morning. There are several shops I want you to see."

Chapter 8

With Ivy Mac heading back to Mobile today, I decided to treat Miss Nella to a chicken finger dinner. I handed her a foam box I had gotten her a few minutes earlier, I opened mine. The memory marker on my taste buds told me I was in for a treat. Memories flooded my mind of college days and Friday nights after a long day of classes and studying, splurging on a chicken finger meal from our favorite hole in the wall.

I took the first bite, and my taste buds were immediately insulted, confused. What had happened over the years? Maybe my taste buds had matured and refined, but I was sorely disappointed. Nonetheless, it was still edible and hard work had made me starving.

"Miss Nella, I came across an article that Mama clipped about a murder at a convenience store. Isn't that the one that is an automotive place now? That one on the highway north out of town?" I snuggled into the swing on the porch. "Yes it is, such a sad story," Miss Nella shook her head. "What all do you know about this Miss Nella? Reading the article jogged my memory a bit, but I was just a young teenager when this happened. The only thing

I remember is that Mama had told me to be more careful when I went places alone and to always watch my surroundings."

"Well sweetheart, your mama was filtering life for you back then. Y'all had enough troubles to deal with at home. You didn't need any outside worries to trouble you too."

The evening air was quite still, very muggy and thick, but somehow the intrigue of another story kept me there on Miss Nella's porch. I threw my legs back up on the swing and settled in facing Miss Nella so I could see every word she was saying when she returned. She had excused herself to go inside for a moment to grab her recipe box.

Miss Nella came back with the box in hand. Each recipe card in the box contained something that had happened in Stormy through the years. It was not something that anyone knew about, the receipt box I mean. Miss Nella said she had kept it in the kitchen by her other recipe boxes. It jogged her memory when she would pass by each card. We both laughed when she referred to the box as her "recipes for disaster". It was pretty fitting, actually, as most of the cards were about deceit, secrets and sometimes murder.

She thumbed through the cards until she found the one that said 1984 – The Not So Convenience Store. She read over what she had written and broke it down for me. "Oh yes, gosh I remember this happening so clearly now. Thomas was actually near the store when it happened. He assisted the paramedics and got the young man to the ambulance, but he passed away en route to the hospital. It was such a sad situation and even sadder was one of the Baxter boys was accused, convicted and sentenced to life in prison for his murder. The Baxters were a pitifully poor family with upwards of 16 children. From either being inbreds or malnutrition, their brains didn't develop the way they should have. The children were not even able to be serviced at school because their IQs were so low. At the time they went through, schools were not equipped to handle students like this. Do you remember them walking along the roads picking up cans?" I nodded. "They were so pitifully poor. Oh Cacky, I remember their mama saying to the reporters that she was sad that Benny was convicted of the murder, but it was one last mouth that she would have to feed at her house. Benny didn't even realize what they had charged him for. He just knew what his mama told him, and he was happy enough moving to a new home where he got lots of food. It was so heartbreaking.

Unfortunately, those that know the truth will never come forward. They are satisfied with the verdict and the sentencing. Thomas tried to tell the authorities that there was no way Benny Baxter could have concocted a scheme as brilliant as had been laid out, but again turning that blind eye was a common gesture on the behalf of the wealthy of the town. I guess there really isn't anything money can't buy." Miss Nella took a bite of her dinner. I told her to eat first and then finish her story, but she went right on.

"Thomas overheard a conversation that the store owner had with his friend at a party right after it happened. Mr. Drinkard bragged about plotting, following through and planting evidence that would place the blame on the Baxter boy. It made Thomas sick to his stomach. Bryar Drinkard had been wanting Samuel's girlfriend for a long time. He was twice her age, but he knew if Samuel was out of the picture, he could convince Marily with his money flashed before her.

Marily was so devastated by Samuel's death that she moved north after graduation. As far as I know, she never came back to town. I'm sure it was just too painful.

Bryar Drinkard moved on with his life, married one of Marily's friends from high school. He took an innocent life and never had to pay for it. Only a monster could do such a thing. Stormy seems to breed these monsters. I'm glad you were able to get away, Cacky," Miss Nella said as she paused the story for another bite." "Me, too Miss Nella, me too! I know there are people like this everywhere, but Stormy does seem to have a large share of people lacking a conscience.

An older cousin of mine told me years ago that when she was a little girl, she went with her daddy to sell cotton. It was a long wait usually to get the cotton weighed. They had been in line for hours, along with many others. A black man was in line ahead of them. A man of great wealth came to the front where the black man was, shot him dead, moved his body out of the way and got his spot in line. If you witnessed this murder, you knew what was good for you and your family, you just kept silent and moved on in the line. I guess monster breeding has been in practice for a long time here. I'm pretty sure it has. Mama had some stories too," I said letting Miss Nella take a few more bites.

"Samuel was a young man that was really going somewhere in life. He didn't have anything given to him. He was a good-looking young man. Reading in his obituary, he played football, was in the FFA and a smart and industrious boy. He had already started getting ready to go to the trade school to be an electrician. He had saved up enough money for his first year by working at Mr. Drinkard's store.

Thomas went to visit Samuel's mama after the funeral, and she had shared so much with him about his future and the plans he had made. It broke her heart to recall everything, but she was grateful that he allowed her to share about him. It was comforting too."

"Is Samuel's mother still alive, Miss Nella? I know she still grieves if she is. I cannot imagine losing a child like that. "Yes, I believe she is. She would be in her 70's now, but I'm pretty sure she is still living."

"Well, I would love nothing more than for Samuel's murder to be reopened, and have a real investigation, but I'm sure it will never happen. How many more murders happened that we just don't know about, Miss Nella? How many monsters have killed people and gotten away with it? How do they live with themselves? This just really makes my blood boil," I said through gritted teeth.

"BOOM!" Lightning struck close to Miss Nella's house. It almost sounded like a gunshot, but the flash gave its origins away. Malcolm zoomed inside, leaving us on the porch scrambling to get things tidied up and put away before the rain started. Miss Nella grabbed her recipe box and headed inside. Thunder pounded again as I descended the steps and made a dash for Mama's house, filled to the rim with things to process during this stormy night. It made for restless sleep, and I kept replaying Samuel's story in my head, shedding quite a few tears thinking about his poor mama and the grief she must still be bearing.

Chapter 9

Getting an early morning start I headed over to Miss Nella's for breakfast. I had errands to run in town today and since it wasn't a court day for out-of-towners, I could drive my car in town. "What a luxury that will be." I thought.

"Didn't you graduate with Sarah Elizabeth Warren?" Miss Nella asked as she poured me a cup of coffee. "Yes, mam I did," I said as I reached out to get my favorite mug from her. "You ever hear about what happened with her?" Miss Nella pulled out her notecard to make sure she got all the information correct. "No mam. I hadn't heard anything about her in years. I know she married late, but I don't think I've heard anything else. What happened? Is she still living around here?" I asked rousing my listening brain into motion. "Well, sort of. She is up at the women's correctional center near Atmore. It was a horrible thing that happened. She married late, yes. She was a bit obsessed with her husband. She did everything for him, was a bit too proud to be married to him if you asked me. She was about thirty when she got pregnant. She had a darling baby boy, name Alex. Oh, he was so cute. Still is for that matter. They were the perfect storybook family, it looked like. They would walk in the evenings around the square together and looked so happy."

"His mother, oh what a dear, she had cancer. Since his daddy had died a few years back and he was the only child, he started spending more and more time helping with his mom. In Sarah Elizabeth's mind he was neglecting her and not giving her the attention she felt that she deserved. Well, she started seeking attention elsewhere. I don't mean she had an affair. Her obsession with her husband was too deep. She started drawing the attention back home. Have you ever heard of Munchausen's Syndrome? Well, it was sort of like that, but she was projecting the illness on her child.

She started slowly poisoning Alex, little bit here and there, thinking it would work quickly, and focus Jackson's attention back home quickly so she wouldn't have to continue. It would usually coincide with his visits with his mom or if he was taking her to a doctor's appointment.

These crazy episodes of the boy being ill, made her husband worried sick, but they always coincided with his mom's visit and he felt torn. At that point he chose to help his mom, because she didn't have anyone else to help her. Jackson knew in his heart how much Sarah Elizabeth loved their child and she would take good care of him while he was with his mom. This went on for about a year until his mom passed away. The little boy was in bad shape by that time"

"The day of his mother's funeral, she decided to up the dose hoping Jackson couldn't go to the funeral. This landed the child in the hospital. Her maniacal behavior had gone too far. The morning of the funeral the child was listless and barely holding on. She tried to call her husband, but his phone was off for the funeral. She called others, leaving a message with half a dozen people she knew would be attending the funeral and no one had them on. Infuriated that she had not disrupted the funeral, she decided to drive the child to the hospital, she knew she had gone too far this time.

The hospital staff noticed upon their arrival the state which the mother was in and chalked it up to a worried mother who didn't know how to express herself. One of the nurses felt very strange about her actions and behaviors and made note of them, not being able to put a finger on what was rubbing her the wrong way. The medical staff took Alex back for assessment. They ran many tests but couldn't figure out what was going on.

When the funeral was over his dad got the messages and rushed to the hospital. Frantic, they let him back to see his son and wife. Worried, he ran to hug his wife who then fully kicked into worried mother mode and wept dramatically into her husband's chest. His shirt was dry when she pulled back from him, he didn't even notice, but the nurse did. She knew something wasn't right.

His bloodwork had come back without any infections or anything. The nurse pulled the doctor on duty to the side after a bit and asked that the little boy remain in the hospital for a few days. The doctor agreed that they should monitor the situation. She hadn't mentioned the irrational behavior of the mom.

Sarah Elizabeth sat by her husband's side as he held the hand of the little boy and wept pitiful tears. He had just lost his mom and now this. He appreciated the abundant comfort that Sarah Elizabeth seemed to be providing.

He got up to leave for a moment and the nurse caught him in the hallway. "He is a sick little boy, Mr. Sullivan. I believe we are going to get him in a regular room and keep a watch on him for a few days." "Yes, thank you. That would be a great idea." Jackson agreed in such a weak voice. Melanie, the concerned nurse bowed her head gently in deep empathy as she slipped away to perform the rest of her duties on her shift. "I will be back in a few minutes," she offered. Jackson stood outside his little boy's triage room and prayed, asking God to help the medical team find out what was wrong so his little boy would have his health restored.

As he approached the room, he saw his wife on social media showing pictures of Alex and asking for thoughts and prayers. He thought it strange to take pictures of him in this condition but would welcome any and all prayers at this point. So, he didn't say anything to her. He moved back closer to the bed and held his son's hand again as the little boy stirred. He smiled faintly at his dad as Jackson wiped the tears from his eyes with the hand that wasn't holding Alex's. He hated to see him with all these lines and tubes everywhere.

"I'm going to be alright, Daddy. Don't worry. I feel the same as I usually do when I get sick. It just is more this time." He squeezed his hand as he looked over at his wife who was deep in conversation with multiple people, neighbors mostly who were wanting to help. "Sarah Elizabeth, Alex needs you," Jackson said forcefully, almost angry. "Put that up for now." "Just a second. I have one more message to type," she said almost shooing him away. "Here, I will do it for you." He grabbed the phone so quickly she didn't have time to act. She certainly wasn't anticipating this. She reached to grab it back, but he was quicker and stronger. Sternly he said, "Be with Alex." He went to her messages and messaged the last response needed from the neighbors. He closed out the messages and went to look up the funeral home's number to give them a call. He had forgotten his phone in the rush to get into the hospital and wanted to make sure everything had been taken care of. He pulled up the search engine and flinched, almost gasped, but decided to stifle it. The last page she had visited was a website about poisoning, dosing and results. He took a screenshot of the page, sent it to himself and then deleted the message. He was in shock. His knees were so weak, his face hot, his breathing shallow. Was Sarah

Elizabeth poisoning their son all along? He went back and sat with Alex again, praying that he would be okay. The doctor came in. He talked to them about what a mystery these symptoms still were. Alex apparently had a bad reaction to something, and they would like to keep him for a few days for more testing and observation. Sarah Elizabeth jumped straight up in open defiance, "I think he will be okay to go home. I can take care of him, and his dad can stay home from work for a couple of days so we can care for him around the clock." The doctor did not agree to this, and Jackson agreed with the doctor. With counterfeit comfort as to not alert his wife that he knew, he kept his arms tightly around her. Alex would be in excellent care there and certainly be away from her. He knew at this point that his being here would save Alex's life.

    Against anything he thought was logical he said he was going to get coffee and left to go talk to the doctor. He told him about the website he had found and asked if it could be poisoning. He asked for confidence in the matter. The doctor said he would chart it but keep it quiet while they ran more tests.

Melanie was stunned when she saw the note appear on the screen in Alex's chart. "Suspect poisoning. Test to be run," she whispered aloud. That was it! She knew that it seemed familiar. Last year when she went to the beach for vacation, she took several mystery novels with her to read. One of the novels was about poisoning. The little boy's reaction to the poison presented the same way as the person in one of her books, only they didn't make it. She got up quickly and went to tell the doctor. They began to run tests for poisoning that day and sure enough it was just that.

They admitted Alex to a regular room, flushing out the poison as quickly as possible and keeping him for a few days would let the poison get out of his system completely. Encouraging Sarah Elizabeth to come home and get a nap and shower was not difficult, if Jackson went with her. Knowing that Alex was cared for, Jackson agreed to go back to the house. With the police chief being alerted, Jackson had sent the police chief a text as a signed release, allowing them to search his house. He made sure they would delay their trip home long enough for the police to have time to search their home. There were people still there tidying up after the funeral dinner. The police entered and sure enough she had hidden the poison among her makeup containers in the top drawer in the bathroom.

Before they went out of the room, Sarah Elizabeth's phone rang. She answered, "Hello. WHAT? Why are they there? Where are they in the house? What are they doing?" She was frantic at this point, completely looking like a crazy person. The person on the other line was dumbfounded by her reaction and didn't say anything else. Sarah Elizabeth threw her phone across the room, and it smashed into the wall. Alex was so frightened he started crying. "What's wrong Mommy?" "Nothing Alex, go back to sleep!" she yelled at him. Jackson had never seen her like this before. She got her purse, ran out of the room and tried to run down the hallway, needing to get away before the police could find her, but fortunately the police chief had sent one of his officers just in case this happened.

Jackson heard the raucous out in the hallway, the screaming, the struggle and then heard the clink of the handcuffs and sank into a chair and bellowed a cry of despair, of loss and almost losing his son too. He jumped up to move closer to Alex, squeezing his hand.

With the arrest made right then and there, she was taken to jail and was left there to await her trial. It was highly publicized, high-profile and a very quick decision was made by the jury. Alex wasn't present but his before and after pictures were projected, allowing the jury to see what had been going on. Alex was thriving now with his dad being in charge.

When the jury handed over the decision, Jackson gulped down tears and looked up. "Thank you, Lord for sparing my child!" The entire courtroom erupted in "Amen!" It was something I had never experienced before in a courtroom, and it was beautiful. Oh, Cacky, that was the most horrific thing I could ever imagine! I'm thankful that Jackson did a tell-all to the press and I got to be there in the courtroom for the specific details. Maybe his testimony will save another child's life. I sure hope so." Miss Nella concluded as she replaced the obviously wrinkled note card back in the box. This was one of the most difficult stories that she told. I understood completely. I could feel the wrinkles of that notecard in my heart.

Chapter 10

Tuesday's breakfast was delicious. Miss Nella made scrambled eggs, bacon and a yummy cream cheese coffee cake. Such wonderful nourishment for the workload ahead of me today. I had been up early this morning and was ready for it.

"Miss Nella do you know Madeline Nauser?" as I sat down. "No ma'am not exactly. I know a Michael Nauser. Is that maybe her husband? Nauser isn't a common name around here. Michael worked on some deeds for me on some property I sold north of here. "Well according to Mobile news he's gone missing," I told Miss Nella.

"What in the world?" said Miss Nella as she scooted forward in her chair. "Did they say what happened?" she continued. "No, not much. Just that he had gone with his wife to a conference in Seattle, and after a whale watching excursion, he had gone missing. I'm sure the buzz will be about town. I'll keep my ears open and let you know if I hear anything," I told her.

"You know, Cacky," she continued. "Oh yes, wait a minute, I know exactly who Madeleine is. She grew up in the country a good piece north of here, in an affluent family. She became a hot shot attorney. That is where they met, in law school. From what I understand she is quite a bully. I think he ended up quitting his practice because she constantly belittled him about the local cases he took. I heard them on the phone one time when I was in his office. She was so mean to him, but he took it all with a grain of salt. I reckon that would wear on you if you heard that day and night. It's a wonder he stayed with her this long. Most of his family is gone now I believe. They were from Kentucky. They left him a hefty fortune. Maybe he disappeared on his own. I suspect I shouldn't speculate about such an event. I guess we will see how things unfold."

"Speaking of stories unfolding, how was Nola Mae when you went to see her? You know I don't like you going over there," she completed her monologue.

"Nola Mae was beginning to open up with me today, until Mr. Blankenship showed up. He is evil to the core. He just shows his face and it's like a spell is cast on Nola Mae. She immediately gets silent, cowers and begins trembling. I know there has to be a traumatic event connected to him. I have even seen students who do the same in the presence of abusive parents."

"I left her after thanking her for the pleasant conversation and told her I would be back to her house at 10:00 this morning. Mr. Blankenship wouldn't suspect that I would return a second time during the day and maybe he would be at work instead. I told Nola Mae that we would have to switch up the time every day so Mr. Blankenship wouldn't know when I was coming over. "He can keep his meddling presence away long enough for me to talk to you." I told her. So, I'm going to stop back by the bakery and pick up some doughnuts for her. Do you want me to pick up some for you too? I asked Miss Nella. "Oh yes, please. I have a group of ladies joining me for afternoon porch chat. You are coming today, aren't you? Maybe get me a mixed dozen and Cacky," she warned me, "Please be careful. Mr. Blankenship is a powerful man who usually gets what he wants by any means that he sees fit." "I promise I'll be careful, but this whole business with Nola Mae has me worried something awful. I will let you know how it goes when I bring you your doughnuts." "Okay, sweetie, call me if you need me." Miss Nella offered. "Yes ma'am, I will."

Walking back to the house I doubled my steps almost running. I was very much looking forward to meeting with Nola Mae again. I felt that if she was out of Mr. Blankenship's sight, I might get some answers.

Sweet B's Bakery was busy as usual and I had to park behind and go through the rear entrance, which was fine by me. Taking a little paper number, I knew that my wait would be a few minutes, so I checked my delivery status on some things I'd ordered and poured a cup of coffee. "79." "Yes mam, right here." My order was filled and excitedly I was on my way. I drove around to Nola Mae's house but parked at the library and walked down from there. She was there promptly at ten and we sat on her side patio. Not much had changed since the 1970s on that patio, but she had managed to keep it clean and tidy. Well-made patio furniture had a way of keeping its youth. We sat and enjoyed our treat. Just being around her made me feel like I was with one of my 4th grade girls. It was like she had frozen in time at ten years old. I tried to think of things to talk about like I would with one of my students. I asked her what she liked to do all day. She told me she liked to keep the flowers watered, play jacks and read books. She told me she had a library card and went to the library every week. We talked some more and she told me she would like for me to come back tomorrow. She would like to show me some of the books she was reading. I agreed and began walking back to the sidewalk when a red truck pulled up and drove purposely very slowly by as if warning me to leave. Decaled on the passenger door was Blankenship Garden Center. I let out a guttural noise, disgusted and walked the other way. "What an imposing jerk!" I thought. "Surely he had other things to do than to keep tabs on Nola Mae and my visits."

    I headed back over to Miss Nella's laden with wonderful treats from Sweet B's. "Well, how did it go?" Miss Nella asked. "It went really well. We had a wonderful conversation about all the things she loves to do. She is precious, Miss Nella. Nola Mae is stuck back at ten years old as if she was stunted emotionally at that age. You know that is a real condition, Miss Nella? It's something called arrested psychological development. But she was very happy to have a visitor and I plan to continue my visits." "Did Mr. Blankenship make an appearance?" asked Miss Nella, all mother-like. "Yes, but only as I was leaving. He slowly drove by where I was walking. I suppose he thought it was intimidating. I thought it was annoying. I made a date to go back tomorrow to see Nola Mae and discuss her favorite books." I added

"Okay, now Cacky, you have to promise me you'll be watchful. We don't need you to go missing like Michael did." Miss Nella gave me a stern look.

"I promise Miss Nella. He doesn't seem extremely maniacal but apparently has some unnatural hold on Nola Mae. I may or may not find out, but what I do know is that my conscience cannot allow me leave this alone. Nola Mae needs help. She needs freeing from the binds that Mr. Blankenship has applied. I want to help her.

All afternoon I kept thinking about Nola Mae as I painted baseboards and cleaned bathrooms. I kept thinking about the age when she seemed to be stunted and what could have happened so badly that it caused this psychosis. I decided to take a break and sit down for a bit. I scrolled through my phone getting updates from all the people back in Kansas City, along with emails I needed to check and respond to. While scrolling, I happened to think about Nola's emotional age and made a timeline to see if it would help lead me in the right direction. Fortunately, my cell carrier had a strong signal, because apparently Wi-Fi here in Stormy was lacking and unreliable. I got my notebook that I had been writing notes in for my next book, pulled out a clean piece and began my timeline. "Let's see if Nola Mae is sixty, that means she was born in 1964. If she was stunted at ten years old, then something must have happened in 1974 give or take a year.

A knock at the door startled me. Why was I so jumpy? I laughed and got up to answer the door. A rough looking character was peeking in windows on the south side of the porch. I opened the door and let myself out onto the porch.

"Hello mam, my name is Billy Holmes. I'm just looking for work and thought you might need help with your yard. I agreed to an amount, and he started to work. He worked for a bit and then made himself comfortable on the porch. I went outside and gave him a bottle of water. He was thankful. We started talking and he told me he was a born again Christian but still had problems trying to stay on the right path. He said he had a problem with the demon liquor. He talked for a bit, and he found himself telling me all about his problems. I certainly didn't mind listening, and we ended up talking scripture, recovery and how we were both thankful for grace and mercy.

He started crying, "Ma'am," he said through his sobs, "I need to tell you something." Goodness I couldn't imagine there was anything else to tell. "What is it, honey?" This reply sent him sobbing harder. "What is it?" I said again very motherly. He calmed down and said "This man handed me this note, called me a ne'er-do-well and gave me $200. He said to come to this address and slash the tires on your car. I guess I got greedy when I thought about the money and even the possible jail time. At least in jail I'd have food and a place to sleep, but ma'am I can't do it. It would be very wrong of me. You listened to all my problems and prayed with me. How could I do that to you?" He began to cry again. "I tell you what, you give me that slip of paper, keep that money and go get yourself some food and a hotel room. Here's $50.00 to add to your stash. I won't say a word about you taking up the offer. Just make yourself scarce so the man doesn't find out you didn't do it. Hey, do you know who the man was or at least what he looked like?" I asked Billy. "Oh, yes mam. He's a very angry looking old man. His eyes are so strong if you know what I mean. He scared me a bit" Billy said. "Well, you run along, and we'll pretend this never happened." I shooed him off lovingly. "Thank you, mam. God bless you." "You too, Billy. You, too."

Holding on to the paper he gave me tightly, I walked to the end of the porch. I watched from the south side as he walked back toward town. I looked down at my hands and saw that I was holding the paper so tight my knuckles were white. I turned and walked slowly into the house locking the door behind me and collapsed in a chair at the table, shaking. This had affected me more than I realized. I don't break easily, and this about did me in. I got my glasses on and read the note. The edge was dirty, and something was scribbled on the backside. Crepe Myrtle - two dozen. "Well good grief, at least he could have used a less damning note card. This was directly from his garden center.

After all of that, I'm sure not feeling like eating dinner. I got a cool shower and headed to bed. Sleep proved to be difficult tonight. Every noise that was made, echoed throughout the 14-foot ceiling, not knowing where to land. Every moth that encircled the porch light, shadowed large creatures dancing on the walls.

Morning light was quite welcomed. I got up to let Maisy out, brought her back in and headed out back through the back door and down the path to Miss Nella's for morning coffee and breakfast. She was already out and about in her garden. She was so excited about getting her delivery from the garden center the day before, she had been digging since daylight.

I waved a cheerful good morning, and she got up off her kneeling pad and headed to the porch. I followed closely behind knowing she would have a large thermos of coffee waiting on the porch. "Have a seat," she said. I sat down and made myself comfortable. Miss Nella brought me a mug of coffee and fixed me a plate of fruit and banana nut bread. Boy, that brought back memories. It was just like when I would come sit with Miss Nella as a teenager, discussing mean girls at school or boyfriends. She would usually have some kind of cake, cookie or muffin. Miss Nella, I don't want you to be scared and I promise I'm going to be careful, but I want to tell you what happened yesterday afternoon." I recounted the incident with Billy Holmes. She wasn't surprised that he gave in and couldn't go through with slashing my tires. "I think he does stuff just to get put in jail so he can eat and sleep there, poor boy." Miss Nella said sadly. "But what upsets me is someone would have even put him up to that. Do you know who it might be?" "Well, I do have some leftover enemies from high school, but you would have thought they would have grown up by now," we both chuckled, me trying to make light of the situation. "No, really do you think it might be Mr. Blankenship?" Miss Nella asked. "Yes, I do. By the description he gave me and the paper with my address on it, having scratched out plant orders, I would assume. But I'm not sure totally.

"I told you to be careful!" Miss Nella narrowed her eyes sternly at me. "Oh, I most certainly am. Can I take some banana bread to Nola Mae today, pretty please?" I asked politely. "You sure can. Take her the rest of the loaf. I'll make some more later today."

Miss Nella generously offered. "Thank you, Miss Nella." I reached down and squeezed her hand, like I do. "I'll report back in later this morning after I go see her." She gave me a smile and a nod.

Again, I parked down the street, but in clear view of the patio where I was to meet Nola Mae again. She was outside watering when I walked up. We walked out to the patio and had a seat. Nola Mae had stacked up all her favorite books on the table. I could see the well-worn spines. Presenting her with banana bread made her squeal with delight. That was apparently her favorite treat. She enjoyed a slice while I looked through her stack of books, mostly Beverly Cleary books. But Nancy Drew was also sprinkled in. She obviously had read them many times. "You like to read a lot?" I asked her. "Oh, yes. I can escape to another world when I read. This world is too hard sometimes," she said wiping the crumbs from the corner of her mouth. "I know exactly what you mean, Nola Mae." She froze. She looked really puzzled at me, moved closer and whispered, "You saw it too?" and then gasped. "I saw what, Nola Mae?" and then she got really quiet. I knew I needed to end our visit right there for today. "Nola Mae, can you take me to the library sometime?" I asked changing the subject completely. "Sure, that would be great!" Nola Mae smiled excitedly and I was relieved my redirection was successful. "I have to work at Mama and Daddy's tomorrow, but Friday you and I can go book looking." She seemed to like that idea. "See you then!" I said as I walked off expecting to see Mr. Blankenship minding my business. But there was no sign of him. I drove home and parked. I walked back to town feeling like we had had a breakthrough. I trotted off to Mother T's for lunch. I couldn't wait to taste her collards and mac and cheese. Something I've been craving.

Chapter 11

Making it the six blocks to Mother T's downtown on the square wasn't too bad today. I had just had my fill of delicious southern cuisine. Satisfied and happy I started to make my way to the door. Mother T's place had windows all across the front of the restaurant leading to the street. Substantially replenished, I walked slowly, finally reaching the front door. A few people were entering, and I held the door for them. I looked up to find Mr. Blankenship heading my way. He wasn't paying attention, so I slipped behind the door that I was holding, pretending to practice my southern manners. Thankfully he continued to be preoccupied as I stood behind the door holding it open for the flood of characters heading to satisfy their midday hunger.

Court must have just let out, I thought with the flood of customers filing through the door to Mother T's. That left only Mr. Blankenship walking down the sidewalk. No doubt he was headed to his garden center. Who knew what was on his mind, that he was so absent mindedly walking towards his place of proprietorship that he didn't even see me. The morning was humid and as noonday arrived the sun had only dissipated a small portion of the lingering droplets. As he passed by, I breathed a heavy sigh of relief only to engulf an entire breath filled with a lovely cologne that Mr. Blankenship was wearing. I thought that might be the most positive thing I can say about Mr. Blankenship. He smells good. After mapping that wonderful scent and positive thought into my brain, I turned in the opposite direction of where he was heading and walked toward Mama and Daddy's house.

Passing all the familiar places on the way home, I stopped in at the Tipsy Cricket. Though no longer the gas station, they still kept the fountain drink machine and made tea daily. I knew with all the work I had to do this afternoon I would need to get a sweet tea to keep me going.

Walking to the back of the store where the fountain drink machine was located, I marveled at the shelf after shelf of liquor and wine. This would have never been something I would have seen growing up in this dry county, but I guess times have really changed. So much has changed.

I made my purchase and headed out of the building towards home, sipping slowly on my sweet tea, knowing it would need to last all afternoon. Once inside I immediately went to check on my faithful companion Maisy. She traveled everywhere with me and was happy just to be there. She was going on twenty years old and had been passed down to me from Mama after she died. I secured Maisy's harness and opened the front door to walk her out. She was quite eager to find a potty place amidst the pinecones and rogue wisteria vines that had made their way into the grass. Completing her business, we headed back inside to check the list of what was on the docket for us today. We settled down on the sofa. I pulled the pen from behind my ear, thoughtfully glancing at the enormous list that lay heavily in my hand. Sensing my overwhelm, Maisy crawled closer to me and making sure she had made contact, settled in by my side.

I jerked suddenly, startling Maisy. Where was that smell coming from? Can something be so lovely and so terrifying at the same time? Mr. Blankenship's cologne was quite present. I waited a few seconds before rising to search the house. Surely, he wasn't in my house. I had just seen him walking towards his business. The scent grew fainter when I left the room and I felt it was futile to continue the search. Maybe I was imagining. I went back into the den and sat down. Maisy hadn't offered to join me on the search, so she stayed right in the position where I had left her. That familiar smell returned. I thought at that point I had gotten my sweet tea out of the wrong dispenser at the Tipsy Cricket, and wasn't in my right mind, but I knew better. Maisy stirred and the smell was even stronger. I leaned over and smelled her and almost passed out, not from fumes but from fear. Maisy's head was strong with the scent, the cologne that Mr. Blankenship was wearing. But how? She had been in all morning, which meant only one thing. Mr. Blankenship had been in my house! My blood was boiling at the same time I had freezing shivers come over my body. He had been in my house and petted my dog. The violation that I felt was evident in my face and body and I had to cool off before I did something rash. This only fueled my determination to find out what was going on. What happened with Nola Mae? Why was he so angry with me? I needed to find out more from Nola Mae before I went to the sheriff about him. Nobody acts like she did in his presence unless something had happened. But if he thought he was going to scare me off, he had another thing coming!

It was too hot to take Maisy with me, but I gathered my purse and keys and headed to the hardware store to buy and install a camera doorbell. This wasn't a game to me, but if it was to him, I wasn't going to lose. Nola Mae was worth it, her peace and her life. I would do this for any child, Nola Mae was stuck emotionally at the age when the trauma occurred, and it made her a child in my eyes. I had to find out what happened and set her free. Having installed my doorbell camera, I was satisfied with another layer of safety. Even if someone knows I have one, maybe they would be less likely to break in again.

After book looking with Nola Mae, it would be a few days before I would see her again. There were lists I just needed to check off. I had to get some things done. So, this next visit was very important. Hopefully she would release some more information for me to work with. I sure hope so.

Chapter 12

Working so hard on the house, I decided I need a break. I had run to the store to get some refreshments for the fridge. On the way, I passed my old school. The sadness I felt after passing was enough to make me shed a tear. I thought about all those affected by the teachings of that school, and not the academics that I am referring to. To the right of the school is a pawn shop. To the left is a beauty shop. It was situated at the intersection in Stormy that sustains the most wear and tear on the road signs, an intersection that made enemies of neighbors and stronger enemies of enemies. Right in this intersection there sits this quaint beauty shop. It's darling façade had been repaired multiple times as a result of the car wrecks right at that dangerous intersection. The crashes that occurred outside the shop were visible, reportable and litigated. The wrecks inside were none of these until technology came to Stormy. Then a heightened sense of visibility, reporting and with that came litigation. The crimes were different; slander, defamation of character and another one I would learn about this afternoon. Today the door wore a black ribbon, announcing a death. I didn't think about it again until I went to Miss Nella's.

Miss Mary Agee just happened to come by on a different day than the regular porch chats. She was sitting on the porch when I came bounding up the steps like I was a teenager again. I caught myself, but not in time for Miss Mary Agee and Miss Nella to see my child-like skipping up the steps. "Well, what are you so spritely about this afternoon?" Miss Nella asked with a smirk on her face knowing I was a bit embarrassed about my entrance. "Well, Miss Nella, I have had a three-day streak of not encountering "my friend", gotten a whole room painted today and a delicious lunch at Mother's restaurant again. And now I get to see you!" I giggled to push off some of my embarrassment and to redeem myself.

"Well Mary Agee just came over to visit for a while. Sit down with us. Mary Agee was just telling me about a lady that she used to work with that had passed away. Do you remember Martha Garfield?" Miss Nella asked.

"Oh yes mam, I remember her. She permed my hair one time. She could talk your ear off and still really not have said anything. Oh, I'm sorry Miss Mary Agee I shouldn't have said anything. I know she was your colleague." I said even more embarrassed than I was skipping up the steps. "I saw the black ribbon on the door when I went to the mart earlier. I wondered who it was that had passed.

"Oh goodness honey, you are not wrong and I tell you what, I spent years keeping her secrets to keep families together. She was something else. I was just telling Jan Ella about Martha's son, Fuller."

"Oh, I knew Fuller. We went to junior college together. What about him?" I inquired.

"Well, he found out that Gary Garfield was not his dad. He was mad at the whole bunch for a while, but that was nothing new anyway." Miss Mary Agee hesitated.

"Yes mam! He had such a temper, even back during junior college days. I always got so upset when I saw him get rough with his girlfriend. There was always an element of worry in my mind for her. I think he had roughed her up a few times when he got angry

80

with her. He was such a jerk." I said recalling the situation and getting a bit angry all over again. "I'm sorry, go on Miss Mary Agee"

"Well, apparently Matthew Wood needed his hair done quite frequently. Working at the station next to Martha's I remember thinking it was so odd that he came in for so many haircuts. Martha was very flirtatious with anyone, but especially with Matthew. I just thought she was after a big tip. I promise I try to think good things about people, but she started leaving early after every one of his haircuts and I started being suspicious. I asked her about it and she rudely told me to mind my own business. After a little while she started getting sick when she smelled any kind of hair solution, even hair spray. I knew at that point she was pregnant. She didn't tell me or anyone else about the pregnancy. Her husband was due back from Panama City that month. He had been gone for 3 months working construction on Highway 98. I'm pretty sure she didn't tell him either. Once Gary was back home, she didn't see Matthew anymore. Not liking this arrangement at all, Matthew decided he would move to Mississippi and take a job there." Miss Mary Agee let out a big sigh. This story made her sad for so many people.

"As Fuller grew up and made frequent visits to the shop, it was like looking at Matthew, spitting image, Miss Mary Agee remembered smiling. I don't think others caught on since Matthew hadn't lived in Stormy that long. Everyone assumed Fuller was Gary's child. But Gary knew. It didn't matter though, he raised him as his own. Gary was a good man, if not generous. Bless his heart." Miss Mary Agee said shaking her head.

Miss Nella poured me a glass of sweet tea and served me some tea cakes. I nibbled delightedly on them as Miss Mary Agee told the rest of the story, completely intrigued with her retelling.

"Martha came in the shop one day and finally told me everything. She told me that Fuller had a new boss at the paper mill. His name was Matt. His old boss had retired and Matt had moved back in the area to be near his mama since his daddy died. You know they are from Fig's Landing down by the river, don't you?" Miss Mary Agee looked at me. I shrugged my shoulders because I had no idea.

"Fuller was bragging about Matt to his mom, telling her what a great boss he was. He went on saying that you just never know who you are going to get for a boss when someone leaves. Well, if you ask me that was an understatement." Miss Mary Agee laughed.

"Martha told me that Fuller kept saying that Matt looked so familiar." On that word I choked on my tea cake. "Of course he did, like looking in the mirror kind of familiar," I added to be funny. "You are exactly right. Mirror image. Anyway, Fuller was honored as the employee of the month at his work and he and Matt took a picture together holding his award. This went into their monthly newsletter at the paper mill." Miss Mary Agee took a sip of her tea.

"Martha had Fuller over for dinner one night. Fuller proudly showed her his announcement in the newsletter. Martha glanced at it and her knees buckled. She said she had to sit down or she would have fallen down. She told me she couldn't even breathe. She knew exactly who his boss was, it was Matthew. When Fuller said Matt, it didn't even register with her. With all of the melodramatics, Fuller was demanding she tell why she was acting this way. She didn't know what to do except to tell him. After recounting the story Fuller was furious. He asked if Gary knew. She told him she didn't think so, but Gary proved her wrong. Gary yelled from the recliner, that he had known all along." Miss Mary Agee again took a drink and took a break to eat one of Miss Nella's tea cakes.

"Please go on, Miss Mary Agee, what happened?" I pleaded. She hesitated to finish her tea cake and delved back into the story telling the rest.

"Fuller had never displayed such anger in his life, Martha said. It scared her. He told her that she had put his job in jeopardy because of some stupid fling she had long ago. He said some other things to her she said she would never repeat. Martha said she tried to calm him down, but he stormed out. She said he had to tell Matt the truth and Fuller slowly gathered information before telling his boss that he was his father." Miss Mary Agee seemed exhausted in relating the story.

"Goodness Miss Mary Agee, I didn't know all that had happened. That was definitely after I left," I said, still perched on the edge of the swing. "I'm glad that was revealed. I hope it all worked out. "

"Cacky, I think it did. Her husband was relieved. He had known all along that Fuller wasn't his but had no idea who the father was. It had always bothered him. Matthew was delighted to find out that Fuller was his son. Matthew's wife had left him years ago because she thought he couldn't have children. After that, he spent years pouring into his work, not wanting to disappoint another woman. Now he did have a child and was able to build a relationship with Fuller. What a messy way to end a story, happily, but messy." Miss Mary Agee concluded. She was pale with exhaustion from telling the story.

"Yes, mam. It was messy, but I too am glad that at least now they all know. Thank you, Miss Mary Agee for telling me the story. I do like happy endings." I said as I sneaked another tea cake from the plate.

Chapter 13

"Miss Nella the old Dillard Plantation home has been redone. It is beautiful!" I said very excitedly as I walked slowly up the steps to the porch. "Yes mam. Alene McArthur redid it maybe a couple of years ago now." Miss Nella responded. "Who is Alene McArthur? I don't remember that name. She isn't a local is she?" "No, no Sy McArthur is the mill manager at the paper mill. They moved from Connecticut probably five years ago. Alene had a difficult time fitting in here in Stormy, even though they had plenty of money to be considered society. Alene, I think, was bored to tears. She had left all that she knew in Connecticut to come down here to help her husband advance his career. She must have gotten tired of redecorating her house and wanted to move on to something bigger and better. She went looking around the area for houses that were large enough for a bed and breakfast and found Dillard Plantation in need of repairs. That lady has a keen business sense. She started seeing all of the out-of-town traffic starting to come in and knew there would be a need for more than just The Gavel Motel on The Square." Miss Nella said proudly of Alene.

"Miss Nella how in the world do you know all of this?" I asked.

"Honey, you know I don't like all those parties. I always end up in the kitchen with the help or take a stroll through the gardens where we are. Well apparently, I hit the right night for a stroll because Alene had decided she had had enough of Southern society and taken relief in the back gardens of the Huddle Estate. She approached me while I was sitting on a bench and asked if she might sit with me. I patted the seat next to me and she sat down with a heavy sigh. Apparently, she had not been allowed into any of the circles in town and felt like she was living on the peripheral. Oh, I know how she felt and I embraced listening as her story played out in Stormy. It wasn't a pretty story, but familiar as I know you can also relate, Cacky." Miss Nella said, giving me the look of annoyance toward Stormy society.

"Yes mam, I can, minus the having money part. That must be really hard to have money and still not be accepted. It's kind of like when you get a weather warning alert and it says conditions are favorable for severe weather. I guess the conditions need to be favorable to be part of Stormy "society" and being from up north was not favorable. Kind of fitting isn't it Miss Nella?"

She responded with her usual, "Reckon it is, sugar, reckon it is.'

"So, I guess she found the Dillard Plantation for sale then?" I asked anxiously to find out more about the bed and breakfast.

"Yes, the family had all passed away. The matriarch had been the only one left and she passed of Covid during the terrible epidemic in Stormy. We lost so many people during Covid. She had only one child who died in her early years. The estate then went to her sister who was in a local nursing home. She was more than happy to give up ownership of the plantation. Alene got a good deal on it and started working on it as soon as she bought it. She was quite handy with all the work and somehow was able to get a crew of workers from Connecticut to come down and help her out. My guess is they were more than happy to get out of all the tight Covid restrictions still being adhered to up there during the time. They got the place going and had it whipped into shape in about six months.

It is absolutely gorgeous now. Fortunately, most of the old furniture stayed with the house so she mainly needed to upgrade appliances, paint and redo bathrooms. It seemed to keep her happy, busy and motivated. Cacky, why don't we go to see Alene one day? I know she would love to meet you and I will let her tell you the backstory of its "Haunted" status."

"Oh, that would be amazing! I can't wait to hear all about it." I said excitedly. "I bet it is as beautiful on the inside as it is outside."

"Let me give her a call real quick and we can set something up. Let's go in the house so I can call from the kitchen phone." Miss Nella led the way. We walked through the long and wide hallway, with its gorgeous staircase positioned right down the center. Walking all the way to the back of the hallway and to the kitchen, I sat down while she made the phone call. I felt like a teenager again. There is no telling how many times I had sat down at this very table waiting for treats that Miss Nella would be making for me.

Miss Nella made the phone call. There was just small talk at first, but then I heard Miss Nella asking about us visiting. Miss

Nella's voice went shrill, "Oh that would be wonderful, let me check with Cacky. Hold on a second Alene." Miss Nella placed her hand over the receiver. "Cacky are you available this afternoon?" Miss Nella asked. "Of course I am," I said smiling a cheesy grin, again feeling like a teenager.

Miss Nella uncovered the mouthpiece of the phone and said in her most proper tone, "We would be delighted to join you for tea this afternoon!" And then we burst into giggles, inciting laughter on the other end of the phone line too. It was a beautiful contagious laughter. I needed that with everything that had been going on.

I got up from the table and headed back down the hallway with Miss Nella trailing behind. "I'll pull up and get you about 3:45 today and we will head over. Thank you, Miss Nella for setting this up. I cannot wait to hear all about it being "haunted".

Walking back down the path that joined our houses, I felt someone staring. It was odd and I picked up my step. When I did, Malcolm jumped out of the bushes and chased me until I abruptly stopped, realizing it was only him. His beautiful Maine Coon features made it hard to be mad at him for wanting to play a game, but he scared me to death. I reached down and scratched the top of his head. Satisfied with his short petting session, he meandered back down the path to his cool, shady spot under the bridal wreath bush of cascading white blooms. I turned around and walked into the house realizing I hadn't locked the back door. I need to remember to do this every time now that I made a hornet out of Mr. Blankenship. What a pity! Because of my carelessness to lock the door, I found myself looking carefully from room to room, through closets and behind doors. Just wanting to be on the safe side.

Maisy had not left her spot, but she may not have anyway. I didn't smell his cologne anywhere, so I just went on and gave that sigh of relief that my mind needed. I grabbed Maisy's leash and connected it to her harness. She roused about and got to her feet. Her cute little old lady dog prance made me laugh and we went on outside for her potty break.

Heading back in, I took another look down the street, certainly trying to be aware of my surroundings. At that moment I noticed that red truck. The one that had the garden center logo on it. It was Mr. Blankenship! He quickly turned onto the road going in the opposite direction. To have such a successful business, how is it that he has time to be, I almost want to say, "stalking" me? It's really more like trying to terrorize me. It's getting pretty uncomfortable. Heading through the door, I latched all three latches and went back to the back door to make sure it was secured as well.

Apparently, this encounter had not taken away my appetite, but a light lunch was in order because I knew that tea would be an actual meal and I wanted to be able to eat every last taste of it.

Sorting papers and making piles helped to pass the time. There was so much to do here, but I needed to take time to do some fun things to break up the work.

At 3:45 I pulled up to Miss Nella's in my floral dress and sandals. She had on a similar dress and was clutching her purse as she guided herself down the stairs, off the porch. When she got into my car, she opened up her clutch and pulled out a velvet jewelry bag. She untied the string delicately and pulled out a pearl necklace. "You need a string of pearls for teatime today, my dear," she said excitedly. "Oh!" I gasped. "These are beautiful!" I fastened them around my neck and reached over and squeezed Miss Nella's hand.

"They were a treasure given to me by Thomas's aunt. I want you to have them." "Oh Miss Nella I have never felt so special!" "Child you are very special, you always have been to me." I hiccupped-sighed keeping back tears, knowing my face would be a mess if I cried.

Driving to Dillard Plantation only took a few minutes, so I drove slowly around the square. Thank goodness I wasn't trying to find a parking spot. Miss Nella informed me that the town was preparing for a large crowd to be here tomorrow for a murder trial that was coming up from Baldwin County. It was heavily covered by the press. All the media was already buzzing about trying to figure out where the best spot would be to capture important moments of the day. The major media outlets had shifts of people staying with their equipment that had been set up so they wouldn't lose their spots. It looked like they were setting up for a festival instead of a murder trial. It seemed very strange. I'm not sure I could get used to that.

Arriving at the Dillard Plantation, I could hardly contain my excitement. I hadn't been here since high school prom, where Mrs.

Dillard graciously offered up the ballroom for our promenade and dance. It was a pretty place then, but there was an extra bit of beauty that shone through now. Miss Nella said it really showed up better with all the new landscaping. I'm sure that was the difference.

Heading up to the door, I touched the pearls around my neck, smiled and waited for the door to be answered. A kind lady about my age answered the door and welcomed us in. She hugged Miss Nella and extended her hand out to me in a welcoming manner. Her smile was genuine, and she was very glad to meet me. Boy, that was a change in Stormy. Not everyone greeted you that genuinely here.

Dillard Plantation looked incredible! Every inch of the entry was breathtaking. To the right was the parlor. Alene led us in there to take a seat at one of the tables set for tea.

I tried to take in all of the work that she had done. My eyes wandered all over until I caught a glimpse of the mantle. All along the mantlepiece were pictures of all kinds of people, housed in beautifully ornate frames. In the center was a framed certificate that read, "Ghost Hunter's Dream." Alene saw my stare and told me she would "tell all" during tea. I couldn't wait to hear about it all. I then looked at the north wall. It had a set of old pictures and some framed papers. While Alene had left the room to get all the fixins for tea, I got up to look at the wall. Tears rolled down my face as I saw pictures of the slaves that were on the Dillard Plantation, the ones whose blood, sweat and tears built this place from the ground up. They were the ones that kept it running during their time here. There was a tribute letter that accompanied the pictures and papers on the wall. It read:

Oh, precious hands that wore with hard labor, precious souls kept captive. God bless you all for your efforts, your backbreaking work, your contribution, your lingering spirit that has filled this place with warmth, love and care. You are appreciated and your dedication and hard work have not been in vain. Your memory will reside at Dillard Plantation for eternity.

With much heartfelt appreciation,

Alene McArthur

Oh, the love and warmth just completely flooded my soul. The truth in every word rang clearly. What a wonderful tribute to those who labored so tirelessly to build and maintain Dillard Plantation.

I returned to the table just as Alene came back. She looked at my red face and said, "Oh no, are you okay?" I laughed through the final stream of tears and told her yes, but that I had seen the north wall.

She shook her head understanding. Alene told us that she had cried through most of the research. "I have a plaque for the front porch that is on order from a friend in Connecticut. I tried to get the local plaque and trophy shop to make one for me and their response was "No way!". Well, I found a way and I will proudly display all of the names of the slaves on it. It will be directly right of the door where everyone can see it. I'm sure it will draw some animosity from the locals, but their business is not the business I seek so it shouldn't affect who stays here. Now let's have tea and we will talk all about our famous "Haunted" status."

Tea was delicious. All the sandwiches, petit fours, clotted cream and strawberries, scones, crumpets and to top if off, beautiful lavender infused tea that had been imported from France. What a lovely experience.

"So, Cacky," Alene started. "Rumors had gone around town that Dillard Plantation had been haunted for a while. I ignored the rumors thinking that the town of Stormy just didn't want me to buy the plantation as a full-fledged Yankee. When the B and B opened, I had guests that said they heard voices talking in their rooms and people moving around, walking up and down stairs. At first, I too thought it could haunted and started hearing noises in the evenings. I wasn't really scared knowing it was just the house settling more than likely. As I researched the slaves, I started jokingly calling them by name when I heard noises. After about a week of people hearing noises, reviews started coming up on my website with hashtags of #ghosthunters, #ghostbusters, #hauntedbandb, #Alabamaghosts and so many more. Well, I hadn't intended for it to become a national issue, but reservations started streaming in, keeping me booked. Interviews from papers and magazines kept me hopping. Paranormal investigators were bringing equipment in and out on a weekly basis. Some of the specialists found evidence, so I was playing along. About a month into all of the paranormal business, Mrs. Ellie Stevens came to the B and B and told me that she caught her son and his friends acting like they were ghosts of the slaves to scare "those damn Yankees" back to New York. I laughed at what Mrs. Stevens told me and I told her I wasn't going anywhere any time soon and that our ghosts were quite friendly. So, as we would have it, the B and B was honored nationally as a place that inhabited spirits and I have been booked ever since. Townspeople keep telling me I better paint my ceiling "haint" blue, but honestly the ghosts have been more welcoming and friendly than the people of Stormy." Both of us nodded in agreement with a bit of a chuckle.

With such great food and conversation, we hated to head out. Alene made us promise that we would be back to visit again. We were delighted at the thought of coming back.

After dropping Miss Nella off, I headed back home to get a few things done before I headed to bed. All this talk of ghosts had me a bit on edge. I think I have always been more frightened of unpredictable people than ghosts. Our ceiling is "haint" blue, so I tried tucking in tightly and trying to get some sleep. It had been a very emotional day. Every noise, bird, owl, creaking noise of the settling of the house, car passing by or dog barking made me catch my breath. It was difficult to be tucked in tightly and sweating at the same time. The security of the tucking seemed counterproductive in this hot weather. I fell asleep praying and asking for a hedge of protection for anything dead or alive with intentions to harm me.

Sleep was finally sweet, but brief, before sunlight streamed through the window sheers. I got up and got dressed to go see what Miss Nella had for breakfast. She made me promise I would come over every day for coffee and breakfast and I had not let her down yet, nor did I have plans to.

Chapter 14

Porch chat days had quickly become my favorite days since being back in Stormy. I had only been to three, but already felt part of the Porch Chat group, closely woven souls affected by Stormy's undercurrent. Meeting new people, sharing struggles, hearing stories and just sitting in comradery helped make the drudge and exertion of working on Mama and Daddy's house less taxing. It gave me a chance to step away for a bit. I loved sitting on the porch of Miss Nella's house listening to ladies talk. The courthouse would chime several times before we would leave to go about the rest of our day. What a blessing it was. Malcolm, Miss Nella's cat loved it too. He would make his rounds for petting and usually end up next to me on the swing.

Information that was shared on the porch was to never leave. It was understood that it was to be kept form being "whispers on the wind." No one felt that anything would be divulged elsewhere and that was very comforting.

Miss Nella always had a notecard and pen with her on the porch. If she thought something important enough, she would write it down to put in the recipe box. Having done this for years, that box was now tight with stories and newsworthy items of Stormy. Today Miss Essie joined us. I had not seen her since I left and it was so good to see her. She had been working with and for Miss Nella since I was young. I loved her like a family member. Her embrace made me feel guilty for being gone for so long, but in a good way.

Chapter 15

Miss Essie was an amazing housekeeper and cook. People all over town tried to snag her from Miss Nella. Sally Mason Mosley promised Miss Essie one night that if she came to work for her that she would pay the way for her niece, who Miss Essie was raising, to go to college. She promised her ten dollars extra per week than the most she was gonna be paid by anyone. "Dignity ain't never looked so expensive," she told Miss Nella laughing.

Sally Mason Mosley came from a long line of hateful people. That mean streak was a dominant trait and it bled profusely from daddy to daughters. Sally Mason's daddy was one of the town's dentists. He didn't even try to hide his meanness, just ask some of his patients who had fillings put in without him deadening the spot.

Sally Mason got most of the meanness in the family. She could look at you square in the eye and make fun of you to your face, then act like you had offended her by being offended. Sally Mason had been expected to be a lady with her debutant raising and boy she tried to act the part. But, deep down inside she wanted to kick off her heels, put on some tennis shoes and go wrestle somebody. This did not help her disposition. If anything, this frustration was brought out in plain sight on the nearest victim that society allowed. That would end up being the delivery drivers, the housekeepers, babysitters or people helping in the yard and Miss Essie knew better.

Sally Mason Mosely's endeavors to secure Miss Essie has been a game to Miss Essie. One that she liked to play every time she saw Sally Mason Mosely. Miss Essie knew better, but she did like the chase. She kept her upping the ante every time she saw her. All she did was add gasoline to the fire, but to us it was fuel for explosive laughter that would come about when we saw her the next time.

Mama had her fill of the Mason girls growing up, so she wasn't much help in making funny remarks about Sally Mason. Mama had told me stories about them when I was younger. She specifically remembered an incident where Sally Mason "accidentally" spilled red punch on Mama's dress at the junior prom. Mama showed me pictures that were taken that night and there, right there on that picture was the reason Mama got her dress ruined.

Mama looked stunning. Her dress had been given to her from a cousin that lived in Texas. It fit her beautifully. She was adorned in jewelry that Jane Alice had sent to her along with white gloves and a purse.

Sally Mason couldn't stand that Mama looked so beautiful. It made her furious that she had upstaged her at the prom. Mama was going to sing that night. She always sang at their gatherings. She could entertain for hours with her beautiful voice. Well, that night, Sally Mason was going to make sure Mama would not be getting the spotlight. She cornered Mama and said "Oh, I am so sorry!" as she poured punch on Mama's dress. The funny thing about Mama is that she didn't get embarrassed by much anymore. She grew up very poor, and if it could happen to her family, it had already happened so she was used to embarrassment. She just knew what she could do and that was sing.

To Sally Mason's surprise, Mama used a wrap to cover the stain and it just made her look more elegant and grown up. She wowed the crowd that night and Sally Mason never forgave her for that. Everyone agreed it had been Mama's best performance yet.

What Sally Mason didn't understand was that when you are poor, you have to be resourceful, both with things and feelings. And in her reserves, Mama had stored up just enough confidence to make that night of music the best.

I'm glad that Miss Essie can play that game. There wasn't much fun that had ever been attached to Sally Mason Mosely. If it made Miss Essie feel good, she deserved it. She was a good woman and a hard worker and an even better friend to Miss Nella.

Chapter 16

Friday was already here. Time is moving quickly, and I still had so much to do on Mama and Daddy's house. Sissy joined us again for porch chats today. She had been to the last few and she is so sweet. Sissy is also a transplant. The particle board plant brought her family here years ago. It is now defunct and so is her marriage, but she hung in there anyway as she had done so many years. Sissy is a teacher at the local elementary, so of course we had many things in common. We've had great side conversations about the differences in teaching in rural Alabama and Kansas City. We had plenty of stories that have entertained the other porch chat ladies too.

Today was a different day, though. Sissy was in tears when she arrived for the porch chats. "Miss Jan Ella, have you got a spare room that I can stay until I can figure things out? I cannot believe she put a restraining order on me!" Sissy sobbed. "Oh honey of course, bring your stuff on over, I've got more than enough room," replied Miss Nella. "Come her honey," she patted the seat next to her. "Did something else happen to cause her to react this way and for Pete's sake get a restraining order?" Miss Nella inquired gently.

"Well you know Eric moved that girlfriend of his in with us. I came home from the grocery store last week and she had moved all of her stuff into the house. I knew he had a girlfriend, he always has, but I was blindsided when he brought her over to live in our house. I'm in a real predicament. She is making it miserable for me at home. She is so self-absorbed, vindictive and so mean. I just tried to focus on my students and the end of the year, but it has gotten to me. This is the icing on the cake, though. What am I going to do?"

"I know you are upset about all of this nonsense, Sissy," said Miss Nella.

"Except Miss Jan Ella you only know part of it, and I am so overwhelmed, embarrassed and feel so betrayed. Every time I try to say something Eric takes the walking stick and starts walking around smashing things. I have been so scared. His girlfriend Bridget just stands there smirking at me. I have never felt so much like hitting anyone in my life. I've never been that way. I went to school this morning to talk to my principal about the situation and she said that she had already talked to the board about it and felt like having me as a teacher there was a conflict of interest under her leadership. She also told them that her daughter had to get a restraining order against me because I had threatened her life." Everyone gasped at the same time. Miss Nella jumped to her feet. "His new girlfriend is your principal's daughter? How long have they been together? Did your principal know this all along? Oh, I could spit bullets right now, I'm so mad." Miss Nella was huffing and puffing by this point.

"I guess she knew all along. And my guess is that they have been together since Christmas. We had a staff Christmas party at Mrs. Joyner's house this year. Bridget was there and couldn't keep her eyes or hands off Eric. He is always flirting with the young girls, so there was nothing new with that. She was home on break from college and just graduated in early May. Y'all she is younger than our daughter! It's so disgusting!" Her sobs began again. She was completely exhausted from all of this.

"Yesterday, I guess he came to school and told Mrs. Joyner that I was making threats to Bridget. Mrs. Joyner was furious at this accusation and made an emergency report to the board of education. All of this going on behind my back, without me knowing anything. Oh y'all this is so horrible!" She took a deep breath.

"So what did the board do?" Miss Nella asked.

"The board decided to trust the word of the principal without even talking to me. They are giving me the option of letting me out of my next year's contract or do a full investigation. With her mom being my principal, you can guarantee whose side she will be on. It's all so crooked. I'm so sick about all of this," she resigned. "Please don't tell anyone. This is already so humiliating and I'm sure it has already passed through the rumor run."

We all agreed that nothing would be said to anyone about this. "What about your teammates at school? You said you had taught there many years. Have you talked to them?" I asked, knowing that teacher friends were some of the best.

"Mrs. Joyner told me she had already spoken to all of them about it and they were not to talk to me unless they wanted to be part of the investigation." Sissy said.

"That's using her authority and is messed up. I'm so sorry. You can't talk to them, but I can." I said adamantly. She looked at me hopeful. "I will be discreet. Nobody will know. They just need to know you are innocent in all of this. Give me their numbers and I will call." I motioned for one of Miss Nella's cards and her pen.

Sissy wrote down the names and numbers and then offered up a thank you, truly appreciative. When Sissy handed me the card, Miss Nella told her to start getting out all of her things from her car. "You are safe here for as long as you need. We are going to get this mess all straightened out."

My mind and heart were aching. She had lost her marriage, her home and now her job.

It took a bit for the Sheriff to find Sissy as she had come to Miss Nella's. He wasn't quite sure where he would find her. Finally spotting her car at Miss Nella's house, he brought the order to Sissy and apologetically gave it to her. He knew her. His child had been in her class years ago and Sissy was one of their favorites. As sorry as he was, he said that he had a duty to perform. Sissy looked at him and told him none of it was true. He knew what kind of person she was and would do all he could to help her out. He left with his head down, feeling terrible about all of this. "Sissy, I just wish we didn't have proof that you threatened her. That makes my job really difficult." Sheriff Tucker told her.

"Wait, Sheriff Tucker! What do you mean you have proof? What kind of proof? I have never said anything to her like that." Sissy went from upset to total confusion.

"Sissy there are messages that you sent to Bridget threatening her. They were sent from your email address." Sheriff Tucker said.

"Sheriff we will look into this. There has to be some mistake. Sissy is staying here for now. You can reach her here or at the home phone number. Thank you, Sheriff. She will be in touch as soon as she is able to collect her thoughts and figure this out." Miss Nella waved a goodbye to the Sheriff so we could get down to business figuring this mess out.

As the Sheriff left, Sissy immediately went to her email account, looking at her sent messages. And there they were. Two days ago messages were sent to Bridget's email address. "What in the world?" Sissy started sobbing again. "Let me see your phone, Sissy." I gently took the phone from her hand, not wanting to make things worse, but now I was angry. "Does anyone have access to your email besides you? Eric in particular?" "Yes of course he does. He set it up for me years ago. I have had this email address forever." Sissy continued. "Do you think he set me up?" She started the uncontrollable shaking and crying again. "Yes I think he did.

"Didn't you say you just got out of school on Wednesday? "Yes, we had a half day before release." "The time stamp on this email is 10:14 am. Do you remember what you were doing at 10:14 am on Wednesday?" "Well, we had our end of the year assembly during that time. We were all in the gym for the end of the year awards. And Mrs. Joyner has a strict policy about no phones in our possession during assemblies. My phone was left in my classroom." "Do you have any documentation of the time that the assembly was to be held?" I asked starting to put a firm alibi in place for her. "Sure, we have a newsletter that states when the assembly time was. We also were live on social media for parents that couldn't attend the celebration. That should have the time on it too. Everyone knows that we have it at that time. It's been that way for years."

I chuckled under my breath, "Everyone but Eric and Bridget," and we all erupted in a grateful laugh. "You, my friend need to make a phone call to Sheriff Tucker. I think he will be pleased with this news. It is definitely a crime to falsify complaints and I'm sure that the order will be rescinded under these circumstances. I sure hope they will get jail time for this. Mrs. Joyner is also complicit in this whole operation. I hope there is recourse for her too. I would suggest writing a letter to the board today. We will help you with that. You need your name to be cleared."

"I sure hope my name isn't ruined in all of this. It is already embarrassing enough to have Eric be such a player, but this topped it all off. If the restraining order was filed yesterday, it went to print in the Stormy News today. Everyone will know," Sissy said. "Well considering you live in the Litigation Center of Alabama, I would consider a civil suit for defamation of character. That would definitely be appropriate in this situation." Sissy smiled and picked up the phone to dial Sheriff Tucker. "Hey Sheriff Tucker, she said in a relieved voice. "Do you think you can stop back by Miss Jan Ella's? I need to talk to you."

Chapter 17

I finally had the chance to sneak a dinner in with Robin, a cousin that I had grown up with. Hearing her talk about her shop made me very proud to be family. As the night went along, she shared with me some of the struggles she had in Stormy. It was almost hard to believe the way people had treated her, but not really. As I said before Stormy hadn't always treated me well either.

Wisdom comes with age. I had always heard this and I believed it for the most part unless someone proved me wrong. It definitely lent itself to this situation. Running a boutique is difficult. And it not only takes keen business skill, but also communication, foresight, and creativity. Age does not preclude anyone from mastering the aforementioned skills. But most of the time age gives you wisdom to know when and where to promote, to extend your business, and the knowledge that competition can only stay healthy if it stays positive.

Robin has owned her boutique on the square for several years. It's been a struggle fighting through the pandemic lockdown and just general economic freeze that happened at that time.

Anybody that knows Robin knows her absolute skill for decorating and her creative arrangement. She can make a dirty old wheelbarrow look pretty enough to display in a living room. She's just got such talent.

Sales have picked up tremendously since the pandemic was over and so has the harassment and downright meanness. Technology has added to her plight as social media campaigns have been employed by other shop owners to bring her down.

Robin is always there for people. She has given, donated time and expertise, provided outlets for brides to be, moms to be and of course provided venues for local artists and artisans. So why all this negative behavior? Why all of the underlying bashing? Maybe it was just Stormy's undercurrent. Just like everything else. But just like at the gulf, you may get worn out when you fight against the rip current, but if you make it out alive, you are stronger for it.

Robin tried to keep from engaging in this kind of warfare, finding it hard enough to make use of all her waking hours, pouring into her shop at a maximum. At first it was just offhand comments through Stormy's gossip mill. Her shop was only minimally affected by this defunct gossip industry that had been substantially muted by the influx of out-of-towners. Robin's boutique had only profited by the out-of-towners. Where the ineffectiveness of gossip had failed, the other boutique owners started trying to find things wrong with Robin's shop, sending scouts and making complaints to the Stormy City Council about anything and everything. Having no substantiated evidence for their complaints, it became an irritant to the council.

Having exhausted their complaints, they turned to technology. At first it was negative posts on their social media. Then they realized that was only reaching the locals that had liked and followed them. They began reaching out to people to write bad reviews on their business page. This would certainly dampen business for Robin from the out-of-towners. Robin's responses were always heartfelt, even when she knew they were made up. She always replied there must have been a mistake, and she would right that wrong, just come in and see her. Knowing these were not even real complaints she handled it all like a pro.

Stooping the lowest of the low, the other boutiques then turned to accusing her of racial prejudice. Robin couldn't believe it. She didn't have a prejudiced bone in her body. It's a nasty mess when someone can stir something up so big that could harm someone so much.

One Tuesday morning protesters set up in front of her shop, shaming her for her prejudice. Tears filled her eyes the day they came out. Robin's religious training and wholesome upbringing always taught her to do good in return for evil. These folks protesting were not her enemy. They had been lied to and were only acting accordingly. Immediately drawing attention to her store, the Stormy newspaper had a cameraman and reporter stationed there. In true Robin like fashion, she pulled her sandwich board out from its daily storage place and wrote fancifully in chalk as tears rolled down her cheeks. "Blessed are the peacemakers for they shall be called the children of God. Matthew 5:9."

She made a phone call to the local bakery ordering four dozen doughnuts and thirty cups of coffee to be delivered as soon as possible; a rush order. Robin busied herself by finding a folding table in the back, a nice clean tablecloth and a serving tray. She grabbed one of the newly filled vases of fresh flowers and headed back up to the front to add to her supplies. She couldn't stop the flow of tears streaming down her face. She knew in her heart that God would take care of all of this and that her getting angry about it would only prevent her from doing what she knew was right.

The crowd was gathering all along the sidewalks. Her store was set to open in just 15 minutes. She had already experienced rapping on her door and voices chanting outside. Keeping her composure was getting more difficult. The last knock on the door was the delivery guy from the bakery. He looked nervous and flushed. Robin opened the door quickly as he pushed through the crowd. "Scotty, I'm going to need a hundred more doughnuts and about the same amount of water bottles. Can you handle that?" "Of course I can Miss Robin. I'll be back in about 30 minutes," Scotty replied. He now caught on to what she was doing, and it warmed his heart.

Robin opened the door and ventured outside with her sandwich board conveying the only message she had on her heart.

Angry protesters stood on the sidewalk. Many people she knew and she was broken-hearted to see them falling for the deception. Some she knew to be the instigators and others were just blinded by the deception. The sandwich board message was received by many, and signs slowly started going down.

Robin proceeded to set up the folding table, the donuts and coffee. She brought out the fresh flowers and placed them on the table. She made the announcement that none of them could truly believe that she was prejudiced and if they did for them to come talk to her about it. In the meantime, "y'all enjoy some doughnuts and coffee. I have more coming." she said. Slowly passersby began to move along. Protesters dropped their signs and exchanged them for smiles hugs and apologies for being led astray. Many of them shared in the doughnuts and coffee while others broke into singing beautiful gospel songs. What was supposed to be a riotous confrontation turned into revival. I wish I could have been there.

Chapter 18

Heading over for breakfast at Miss Nella's I sported a bandana covering my head, one of my brother's old t-shirt that Mama had saved and cut offs. I hadn't even thought to put on makeup because today was a day of spackling and painting.

Upon arrival I felt a bit embarrassed as Miss Nella was all dressed up, hair teased, color on her cheeks and lips and darling sandals that matched her summer dress perfectly. "Oh my! You look beautiful, Miss Nella. Where are you headed out to this fine day?"

"Well, I have a few errands to run, going to see an old friend at Stormy Manor and then I am obliged to judge at a beauty pageant, Stormy's Summer Miss." She sat down with an unladylike thud into her chair on the porch, sort of in a rebellious manner and guffawed at the thought but proceeded to tell me about her experience with beauty pageants in Stormy.

"What's not to love about beauty pageants?" Miss Nella said snidely. She recalled being in a few herself back in the day and beginning a new story for my breakfast entertainment.

"The funny thing about me winning so many of the pageants was that I didn't come from money. In fact, most of my dresses, gloves, clip on earrings and necklaces were borrowed from older cousins. Back then it was possibly a bit different, who knows but I guess my beauty caught the eye of the young doctor in town." She pursed her lips and started pretending to fluff her hair. Seeing Miss Nella like this always made me laugh. I loved it when she told stories with antics.

"You know Cacky, society dictated much of what you did when you were married to the town doctor, my precious Thomas. And one not so rewarding task was to judge beauty pageants." She ended with rolling her eyes just slightly.

"The first time I judged one I sat staring, trying to keep my mouth from gaping open. It wasn't because of the stunning dresses, the carefully coiffured hairstyles or the elegant jewelry, that was all lovely and worth celebrating. I was appalled at the contestants' lack of beauty. Careful not to say what I was thinking, out loud I bit my tongue."

The emcee began, "Playing tennis and singing are contestant number one's favorite activities. She plans on pledging at the University of Alabama in the fall. Her sponsor today is the first Bank of Stormy, where her father is president."

"Wait," I thought and almost said out loud." Miss Nella continued. "I knew they didn't just qualify her to win because of her sponsor. She was not a pretty girl, close eyes and a wide mouth, not your typical beauty queen. But the other judges were so overwhelmed by her beauty. They were clapping wildly at her entrance and then again at her exit from the stage. I actually got a little queasy with all of their "put on".

"Contestant number seven was a pretty girl, with natural beauty who was going into her junior year. She was tall and slender and walked with confidence. Her sponsor was the local bakery. I heard one of the judges say "Well isn't that sweet?" with obvious sarcastic tones and some fabricated giggles. Their claps were less pronounced for this candidate than mine and they both turned to stare at me. I just shrugged my shoulders and looked forward. The contestants continued to flow across the stage, some natural beauty, some applied beauty, some were never going to be accused of being beautiful. The more candidates that passed through, I started noticing a pattern from the pageant director behind the curtains. She would give a thumbs up when a more lucrative sponsor had been acquired by the girls. Restaurants, hair salons and deer processing plants didn't seem to cut muster. I couldn't believe this was real. It all made sense in Stormy society, but to see it firsthand was surreal. I was disappointed at the end. I was odd man out in the votes. Only two of my picks had made it to the top ten. What an embarrassment to the town to judge beauty by money. I had just hoped none of the final contestants were featured in a larger newspaper in the area. And I hoped that was just another secret that was kept within the town limit. Going home discouraged was a common thing as I judged one beauty pageant after another through the years. I knew my vote didn't count, which honestly was really the only authentic one. What a shame. But today I shall go with the intention of doing the right thing. You never know if someone else will show up to vote like I do. Then the right thing will be done. Until then, it is my duty to honor Thomas and fulfill my societal duties."

"Oh Miss Nella you are such a treasure! Thank you for always doing the right thing and taking on the responsibility of being true and speaking truth. I'm going to head back to the house and begin my day's journey of spackling and painting. Please tell me all about this pageant later." I said as I placed my coffee mug and plate on the tray by the door.

"Yes mam, I sure will," Miss Nella says as she picks up the tray and heads inside for her final freshening up before heading out.

Chapter 19

"Hey ladies," Miss Lolly came upon the porch carrying a bouquet of flowers from her garden. "Hope all is well today with everyone," she said with such a genuine smile on her face. "Miss Cacky, I'm so glad you are back to share in some of our porch chats. Your mama used to love to sit out with us, until she got so ill. I loved her," Miss Lolly came to give me a kiss on the cheek. "She loved you too, Miss Lolly and appreciated your friendship." I smiled.

"Well ladies I have someone I believe is going to join us for porch chats. I hope that is okay with everyone. She has a story to tell and I want her to tell it. She has struggled with hiding a lot of secrets that I wish I had known. She should be here any minute. Oh, there she is. It's Leslie Rowell."

Leslie climbed out of her car. She bounded up the stairs filled with energy and vigor. "Miss Lolly has invited me to come to what she called porch chats. I hope it is okay with everyone that I am come. I don't want to be an intrusion." "Goodness no," Miss Nella said. "You come right on over and have a seat. Miss Lolly says you have a story to tell. Well, we love stories."

Thankful for the iced cold tea that Miss Nella offered, Leslie took a sip and started her story. "Here it goes. Just a few weeks ago I would have been hurrying to close the windows, I did not want anyone on North Lenoir St. to hear my abusive husband yelling expletives at me again. I tried to save face when I could and would tiptoe around him trying not to let on that I was upset. Richard, my husband is the local Presbyterian minister for those of you who don't know. He was a jewel by day, leading his flock and seeming to be the best of all people in Stormy. His charming demeanor, reverent speaking abilities, his ties to the local charities, and that skip in his step that he had when walking downtown to lunch certainly added to his visible attributes. I began to notice his evening walk was a bit brisker and heavier as its purpose was driven from a demon inside that he just couldn't shake. I could see his forceful walk from the front porch. He knew I would be there and he would cut through the greetings quickly to make his way to his liquor cabinet, annoyed at the thought of the greetings delaying his purpose. He salivated at the thought of whiskey burning his throat as it went down. "Foaming at the mouth" might have been a more appropriate description. This particular night, the one Miss Lolly told y'all I had to tell about is a doozy. Apparently, it took all Richard could do to hold up to the pressures of being the minister, the confidential reiterations that he was exposed to daily had gotten to him. He had no idea what he had gotten himself into. These people here in Stormy are a delight by day but hearing the extent of their nocturnal activities and the problems they had caused had brought him to the brink, no, had expedited his condition of being a raging alcoholic. He just couldn't bear it all without the help of his demon liquor. I understood some of the pressure that he was going through. Every night he would be ranting about things while finishing glass after glass, telling me what all he had been given in confidence to him. He would realize what he had revealed and become angry with me as if I had pulled it out of him with some kind of trickery. That was far from the truth as I really didn't want to know. I swore that I wouldn't repeat anything. It was such a burden to know all that I know, a burden that I didn't want to carry.

At first he would just curse, and scream and cry. But lately he had been more aggressive, and the sobs had turned into throwing things at me, blaming me for everything and finally last week he did the unthinkable. He completed his triad, downed several glasses of liquor, threw what was available and then charged towards me screaming and then shoving, and finally he punched me in the face." We all jumped when she said this part. She was such a descriptive storyteller, and we were riveted.

"I was so shocked and bewildered. I had to think quickly, even with what I thought might be a concussion because had seen stars and then blacked out only to see stars again. The only thing I could think of to was to stay calm, have him drink to passing out and then I would sneak out. I slid down the wall covering my head with my hands, slightly whimpered, hoping he would be distracted by his empty glass and returned to the bottle to get his final dosing for the evening before passing out on the sofa. It hurts to recount the story, but it has all worked out, so the pain is beginning to subside. Miss Lolly had heard the yelling, the screaming, the blaming every night and told me when I came over that she felt sorry for me but didn't want to embarrass me by asking me about it. She just continued to be kind and neighborly. She knew at some point I would explain it all to her. This particular night last month, though, Miss Lolly heard the yelling, screaming, blaming, and then there was silence. She told me she began praying for me. She felt her hands tied as far as going over to help. Rarely does one get involved in domestic disputes, especially in Stormy. She knew this and stayed away, but prayer was powerful and effectual. In the middle of her prayer Miss Lolly said she heard a faint, timid knock at the door. When she opened it, I collapsed in relief to the floor and started crying uncontrollably. I was so thankful she was home that evening. Miss Lolly gently lowered her own body down to the ground and enveloped me in her arms, just like a mama would her own child. I remember the exact words she told me that made me know I was welcome with her as long as I needed to be. Miss Lolly said to me, "Hush now, I got you baby. No one is going to hurt you anymore tonight. Just let it out. You needed to do this for a long time." Miss Lolly then got up off the floor and shut off her porch light. She didn't need anyone else nosing into the business at hand. What a smart lady she is," looking over at Miss Lolly so affectionately. I went on to ask "Miss Lolly, can I stay here tonight?" I was so weak and bewildered. Her motherly response was "Oh yes ma'am you can. I got the perfect place for you and I will be right here beside you. You took a pretty good hit to the mouth, let's get some ice on that. You don't worry about anything else tonight honey. Everything will be all here in the morning to tend to. You just settle in." After a while of her monitoring my condition, Miss Lolly felt that I was okay to go to sleep. She told me "Sleep tight my little angel, God is going to take care of everything." And so, I slept tight and woke up to a rapping on the front door. My head was splitting and I felt nauseous.

Miss Lolly answered the door confidently, not knowing the condition in which she would find Richard. Head down low, Richard came in truly humbled and remorseful. He requested to see me. He figured I had gone to Miss Lolly's. Before she let him see me, Miss Lolly said she mentioned a wonderful healing place in Mobile that worked wonders with the demons that swam in those liquors. He promised he would check into it and she showed him to the room where I was still in bed. I stayed with Miss Lolly a few days while Richard made arrangements to check into the "resort" in Mobile.

Richard's promise was fulfilled. That was the only way that I would agree to stay with him. While Richard was on 'vacation', I spent a great deal of time with Miss Lolly. This is when Miss Lolly mentioned the porch chats. I told her this is what I needed and asked to join in. As a minister's wife people see you as a worker, not necessarily a friend. This is just what I needed. I wish I had known about this sooner, but I know things happen for a reason. Thank you all for letting me come and be part of this. I can already feel the love and support." Leslie concluded. We all sighed a sigh of relief in knowing that all was working out. It is so weird how we never know what others are going through. We just never do.

Chapter 20

Robin told me all about this beautiful place, a tea shop called Adeline's. So much was weighing on my mind and heart this morning and I needed to just get away. So, I went in search of this place. Driving around the square I just headed east for a block and found this delightful old house, with a wraparound porch and a beautifully painted sign that said "Adeline's Tea Shop". It was already welcoming, and I had not even stepped foot out of the car.

Entering the shop, I could just feel the worries slipping away. Mozart was playing quietly in the background. I slowly began my tour of the tea shop. At once something moved to my right. It startled me at first, thinking maybe Mr. Blankenship had anticipated my visit there, but how strange that would be. Instead, it was a raspy voiced cat that caught my attention. I turned to face the monstrous sized cat with light green eyes, that begged for a few moments of my time. His extended paws toward me, drew me in. He was completely irresistible. I made my way to the bay window and commenced paying complete attention to him. As I was petting him, I looked up on the wall to the left. An entire wall was brandished with "Surge" merchandise. "So, your name is Surge, huh?" I continue to scratch his head. He yawned a meow as if telling me that was exactly who he was. I looked through the merch and decided on a soft aqua colored t-shirt with his logo on the front. How cute! I scanned a code that sent me straight to his social media page. Apparently he had quite the following. He was definitely worthy of a fan club and I joined in online. The "about" section says that he got the name when he was a kitten. He would slowly move toward Adeline's head and head-but her in slow motion. She wrote that every time he did that she imagined a surge of water at the gulf and named him that.

Surge and I had different ideas of what it meant to stop petting. I smiled when he tried to catch the bottom of my shirt as I moved along. What a precious soul.

Moving towards the tea shop, I stopped to peruse the fancy teas that she had displayed. I was very fond of teas from different places. There were so many wonderful teas that I could choose. I decided on some nice, bagged tea with a citrus flavor to add to my summer collection.

Following the delicious smells, I wandered into the bakery part of the shop looking into the glass cabinets, deciding which treat I wanted to savor this morning. Deciding on fresh herb and spinach quiche and a berry muffin accompanied by a caramel pear infused tea, I grabbed a cozy spot inside, settled in and waited for my order to arrive. This shop was beautiful, every bit of it!

A lady appeared at my table after a bit and delivered my goodies. She introduced herself as Adeline. She started making small talk and I asked her to join me while I ate. Complimenting her on the beautiful work that she had done on the tea shop and the delicious food, she thanked me profusely.

"Well, Cacky (as I had introduced myself to her earlier), it was a rough start here. I don't know if you are from here or not, but Stormy wasn't exactly a welcoming place." I almost choked on my muffin. Laughing sort of, I told her I knew exactly what she meant. I let her know I hadn't been back in several years and totally understood her position.

"If you have a few minutes, I would love to share my story of coming to Stormy," Adeline said. "Oh yes mam! I love to hear stories and this one will be good, I can already tell." I said anticipating her retelling her adventure with the people of Stormy.

"Well, I moved here from Mobile. My husband had passed away and I was trying to gather my life without him with me. It was devastating and everything in Mobile reminded me of him, everything. It became unbearable and so I started traveling around looking for a place that I might relocate and start a tea shop. I have always wanted one. I came upon Stormy on a Wednesday when all the farmers and artisans had brought their goods into town to the market on the square. It was so lovely and just the buzzing around of people, it felt like the right place for me to bring my worries to. So, I found myself coming back every Wednesday for a couple of months and continued to believe that I should be relocating here. There wasn't a tea shop in town and that kind of settled the deal. Goodness, Cacky, I have collected teacups and saucers and all kinds of dishes for years as a hobby. This was a perfect way to use them." Adeline got up after hearing the door open motioning that she needed to head that way.

I sighed as I continued to enjoy my quiche, finishing every crumb. It was so delicious. Admiring all of the florals in the curtains, tables cloths, plates that adorned the walls, I sipped my tea in such a contented state. It was all so comforting. Adeline came back satisfied that she had taken good care of her customer.

"So, I wandered into a shop on the square called The Robin's Nest. What a delightful lady that owns the shop." I smiled thinking of Robin and our dinner the other night. "Yes, she is the best! Robin is my cousin." "Oh, she squealed. She is a huge part of my story of moving to Stormy. Robin and I talked about my moving to Stormy. She was so friendly and helpful. She started looking for places for my tea shop and found the perfect place only three shops down from her own. I made the down payment, put my house in Mobile on the market and started packing my things. You know I never imagined why Stormy was called what it was. I only guessed that it may have had some major storms that had moved through and given it that name for that reason. Soon I found out that it wasn't just meteorological storms that brewed in Stormy. The forthcoming months would have me running for shelter, literally. Oh, hold that thought," Adeline moved quickly toward the bakery counter.

"Okay so where was I? Oh, yes, running for cover." She laughed a bit, but I'm sure it wasn't funny at the time. "I had no idea I was going to endure some of the strongest social weather that I could possibly face. There was no warning about what was going to rear its ugly head in the months ahead. Cacky, we had crimes in Mobile all the time. We made sure our doors were locked, had alarm systems, and really watched our surroundings all of the time. Mobile was still a wonderful place to be, we just knew what to do. But the crimes here in Stormy are different. They are secretive, manipulating, power wielding and very difficult to prove."

Adeline was very perceptive and very right. She had Stormy pegged to a tee! She continued to tell me what happened with her first shop and it was then I realized that her perception was unfortunately reality based.

"After finding the shop, I started working quickly on it to get it ready to set up my shop. It was the old furniture store on the square. Do you remember that place?" she asked me. "Yes, of course! My mom used to go in and buy things once in a while there." I told her. "Well, I remodeled the store. Many hours of work, sleepless nights and countless prayers for stamina and longevity were said. In a month's time I was able to move completely in with my beautiful Surge by my side. You have met Surge, haven't you?" She asked me pointing toward the bay window. "Oh yes, we have been acquainted. He is beautiful and very friendly! What a great idea for the Surge merchandise." I said giving a chuckle at the thought of his own fan club.

Well Robin's husband helped me with some of the structures in the building and made Surge his own padded window seat right in front of the large plate glass window so he could bird and people watch during the day. It was such a perfect arrangement.

I was starting to remember Robin talking about some of this the other night, but she didn't get into details about it. We were interrupted and she didn't get to tell much more about it. But Adeline was doing such a great retelling, that I was waiting for every word she said. In between helping other customers and pouring fresh tea for me, I got bits and pieces of the full story a little at a time. Having become very comfortable with me, knowing I was Robin's cousin, she told me what happened next. It was heartbreaking and I'm not sure, but it probably would have made me pack up and move. But Adeline forced residence here and has been better for it.

She starts the heartbreaking part of the story. "Mary Turner Lloyd had come in a few times. She always flitted through, looking from the floor to ceiling each time, blatantly taking pictures of the improvements. She minced no words when she told me that she planned to put a paint and sip gallery in this shop. At first, I thought she had lost her mind or had some kind of mental illness until I found out she was the mayor's wife. Then I knew she wasn't kidding or crazy. She was just cruel. I suppose she always got her way on everything, and I had just helped her little pet project along with all of my hard work. The last time she came in, she brought paint swatches. I tried to avoid her because her brazen attitude was really upsetting me. She nonchalantly picked a few things out, purchased them and then walked out as if she owned the place.

The following day I received complaints about the bench right outside my door. The paper stated that the color was wrong. At first, I thought this had to be a joke, but it was signed from the City of Stormy. I complied and painted the bench the way they wanted it. Having that violation satisfied quickly, they moved on. A violation was written about my back door locks to the alley way. I needed to replace the locks, or they would be contacting my insurance company. Oh, I cried over this one." She said as she hopped up to help another customer.

Adeline proceeded to welcome more customers, get them seated, ordered and taken care of. It was a few minutes and I had let myself get worked up over her situation. If this had been me, I'm not sure I would have stayed in Stormy, but apparently she found the good in people here. And I'm certainly glad she did.

Adeline approached me again, excited to continue the conversation. "The lock was fixed immediately by Robin's husband. Compliance was met immediately once again. I sure didn't want to lose this place over an insurance matter. Seemingly undeterred, though, it was still eating me up inside. I decided then and there that my tea shop would be successful.

Surge became a local hit. Everyone wanted to come in and pet him. People stopped in front of the window, tapping lightly to get his attention, trying to arouse him from his sunny nap. I had a local t-shirt shop make t-shirts that had his picture on it with his name, Stormy's Surge. It seemed to fit perfectly. Things were going quite well and I thought the complaints were over, but then I heard that Mrs. Lloyd had been in Birmingham helping her daughter with her first baby. Poor girl is all I could think of. It's hard enough being a new mom without having a nagging nuisance there with you. But whatever the circumstance was, she wasn't being a nagging nuisance to me, for which I was extremely grateful." We both laughed a little too hard on that one.

Adeline continued, "But when she got back from Birmingham, oh hold on I will be right back." Putting up a finger telling me to wait a moment, I felt like my elementary students when I stopped reading at a good part. Now I knew how they felt with cliff hangers and I smiled. It was a few more minutes before she returned, but I just continued to enjoy the ambiance waiting for the story to continue.

She returned with another pot of the delicious tea and then continued as she poured me another cup. Anticipating the conclusion of her story, I was very surprised. We were nowhere near the finish line.

"Mary Turner Lloyd had gotten word of Surge's popularity. Green was not her color and jealousy quickly drove her mad. She apparently wielded her power as the mayor's wife to get a notice written from the health department, that said if I didn't remove Surge from the premises, I would be cited and closed down. I'm sure the health department director was as surprised as I was to get this complaint. Many shops on the square had pets that roamed their shops, greeting customers and enjoying the company of the townspeople. It was just all Mary Turner Lloyd could come up with to get me out of my shop. She must have been desperate for her paint and sip gallery to go to this much effort to close me down. Well, I cried, no I sobbed when I got the letter from my landlord that said he was terminating my lease because of all of the violations that

I had been receiving. My heart was broken. I will be right back. Hang tight, Cacky."

Waiting a little more, I pulled out my notebook and wrote the name Mary Turner Lloyd down. I needed to ask Miss Nella more about her.

Adeline came back to my table with a muffin to go. She was wiping her hands on her apron, readying them to tell the rest of the story. One of the things I immediately loved about Adeline was how much she used her hands to talk, it provided animation to her conversations.

"So, I reluctantly packed my things, ready to move somewhere else, when a lady came through the door. She was a sassy older lady who spoke with a raspy voice. She had heard about my run ins with Mary Turner Lloyd and my displacement and wanted to help. She told me that Mary Turner Lloyd had a way of stepping on people and she wanted to help fix this. I immediately recognized her as one of the window tappers that daily came by to see Surge. She obviously had some past with Mary Turner Lloyd and was adamant that she wouldn't be walking on people without a fight. Mrs. Anna Lou Ford handed me her realtor's card and said she was there to serve me. She laughed heartily as she bought up all the Surge t-shirts and had me bag it up."

"Miss Addy, may I call you that? Get your purse and lock up shop. I have something to show you." I could already feel the blessings flowing. Without a beat, we were in her SUV heading east a couple of blocks. I didn't know where we were headed, but I just knew I was going to enjoy this adventure. We stopped at this darling,1940s home. It had a wraparound porch. It was kind of plain, not like some of the other houses on the street with their ornate gingerbread trim or fancy carved corbels. To the rear I saw a tremendous greenhouse. It took my breath away. I asked Mrs. Ford what this was all about and she said this was the perfect place for my tea shop, with complete living quarters upstairs on the second floor. I gasped, clapped with tremendous excitement and gratitude and followed her up to the door. She easily opened it and we toured the house and green house."

"It's perfect!" I told her. Even more perfect than the one I have now. My brain was on overload and my heart completely full.

"Who owned this house and why did they have such a large greenhouse? I'm not complaining. It is just odd to have one so close to town. Mrs. Ford told me that the lady that lived here sold plants from her greenhouse. Come to think of it, her story was very similar to yours. She sold plants for years, about twenty years. She got this greenhouse to expand her business. Old Man Blankenship who owns the garden center undercut all of her customers and drove her out of business. He's a mean old cuss." I decided right then and there that Mary Turner Lloyd and Mr. Blankenship were very similar. She continued the story, wrapping it up. In my mind I was placing Mr. Blankenship in a category all his own in my book, though, but I held my tongue and let her finish. Adeline saw my demeanor change and asked if I was okay.

"Oh yes mam. I am. These people just make me so angry!"

"Well, there are good people here in Stormy too. I promise. See the next day, I arrived to do some more packing. Mrs. Ford arrived at the door to the shop with papers to sign for my new tea shop. I signed the papers, and she went immediately outside. She didn't close the door all the way and I could hear her saying "Y'all come on in. I burst into tears when I saw a stream of people wearing Surge t-shirts that she had purchased the day before. They were all there to help me move and clean. With so much help we were moved out and cleaned up within six hours. As sad as it was, it was truly a blessing to be in this place. So much healing has occurred.

"So Adeline I see that the paint and sip gallery is under reconstruction. I saw the sign the other day. I thought you had already redone it." I said a bit confused.

"Honey, things come back to bite you when you are mean and nasty to others. Mary Turner Lloyd had a successful business as that was a novel idea for the area at the time. I think there might have been more sipping than painting going on in the place. One drink too many and a negligent smoker let her cigarette hit an open container of mineral spirits and up in smoke went the newly customed drapes, the canvases and the sofa setting off fire alarms and the sprinkler system. Forced sober women, looking like drowned rats that they are, came barreling out of the gallery shoving each other." She started to laugh and I couldn't suppress the laughter inside me either.

"I just happened to be having dinner at the restaurant caddy corner from the Paint and Sip Gallery when all this happened. I almost choked on my food. I'm not sure Mary Turner Lloyd learned a lesson from all of this, but I love my cozy tea shop right where it is now. I'm so thankful for the comfortable living quarters upstairs, a bay window for Surge and having met some of the nicest, most caring people in Stormy. I'm also very grateful for the previous owner, whose hard work and sacrifice allows me to now grow my own vegetables, herbs and fruit year-round." She concluded her story.

"You know Adeline, Mrs. Ford's mama lived here." Adeline clasped her hands together and put them to her mouth, tears welling up in her eyes. "Well, all the more reason to make something special out of this place. She never told me this was her place. Thank you for sharing that with me."

"Yes mam, you are welcome. Thank you for such delicious food and for your story. It has brought such warmth to my heart today. I will be back for sure." I got up and reached out for a tight hug, squeezed her hand for a second and bid her good day. What a joyful outcome!

Chapter 21

Having early morning coffee with Miss Nella this morning, I jumped out of bed and stretched, sore from the previous day's work. I warned her last night that I had to be in Mobile at ten to pick up some materials for the house. She didn't disappoint. She called me at six o'clock and told me breakfast was ready. I hurriedly got on some clothes and ran over to her house, making sure I locked the doors before I left. Making quick and light steps I was still thinking about my trip to Adeline's Tea Shop the other day and it made me feel so good to see her outcome be so positive. There was so much going on in Stormy that was not good, seeing more and more of the good, made me happy.

I stepped on every single one of the garden pavers, just like I did when I was little. It felt freeing. Rounding the side of the house I smelled some delicious aromas wafting through the air, onion, garlic, cinnamon. Laid out on the cloth covered table was fresh cinnamon rolls and a spinach frittata, two of my favorites. It didn't take me long to have a seat, pour my coffee and indulge. My eyes rolled backwards to Miss Nella's delight. "Oh, Miss Nella, this is heavenly!" "I knew you needed something substantial to start your day. And I remembered how much you loved these two things. Eat up!" She said with a cheerful voice.

"Miss Nella, do you know Mary Turner Lloyd?" Miss Nella's brow furled, and her look changed completely. "Yes, I most certainly do. She is the most bothersome person I have ever met. She is also one of the meanest, most vindictive women I have ever met. She is the reason I walk the gardens or head to the kitchen with the cooks at social gatherings. I cannot stand to be in her presence. For years she flirted ruthlessly with Thomas. The only recourse I had was to watch the repulsive look on Thomas' face when she was flirting with him. She certainly never was a threat, just such an uncouth woman." Miss Nella ended her tirade with a sigh of disgust.

"Well that corroborates with the story that Adeline told me yesterday about her dealings with her. Remind me to never, ever mess with her." I said not really thinking I ever would.

"Oh, Miss Nella before I forget. I was looking through some letters from my Grandma, to my mama last night. She had written that my aunt and uncle were keeping busy at work at the Kim Auto

Parts Plant. I had forgotten about that place until I read that. Whatever happened to that place? Didn't it employ a lot of the towns' people at some point or another?" I asked before taking another bite.

"Yes, that's another sad story that could have easily been avoided. It was the proverbial shoot yourself in the foot kind of story. Old Mr. Kim was from Korea. He had plants in North Carolina and here. It was a very productive business. Old Mr. Kim passed away, I think it was like 1994 or so, I can't remember the year exactly. Stormy was doing alright at the time of his passing. After his death, management was holding the business steady, waiting on Mr. Kim's son to come and take over from North Carolina. Young Mr. Kim's name was James. He was born in North Carolina and had been managing the plant there since he was twenty-five years old. He moved to town in November, ahead of his wife and children, not wanting to disrupt his children's school year already in progress. James was a very good manager and was fair and kind to everyone. Stormy seemed to have taken the transition well. James had found a beautiful house on the golf course for him and his family. His family joined him in June, when school had let out in North Carolina. I met them at a gathering for the Chamber. They were such sweet people.

James went to Stormy Preparatory School to enroll his children for the following school year. The secretary, with her poofy yellow hair, reluctantly gave him two applications. It bothered James that she reacted this way and he wondered if he had done something that crossed the southern manners line. Nonetheless he went on and filled out the applications meticulously. He did all the things that were needed in order to register them for school. He was really surprised that a school that had preparatory in the name didn't require uniforms, but he let that slide." Miss Nella poured me some more coffee.

"They waited for a response about the enrollment but didn't get one. James called the school after about two weeks of waiting on them. A nervous secretary told him to expect a letter in a day or two as the board had met with a decision. The secretary was correct, and the letter came in the mail on Friday afternoon after the school had closed. He would have to wait until after the weekend to call them.

Inside the envelope was a rejection of admission letter for his two children. The board stated that at this time they were not accepting any new applications for the following year. James, a usually calm and cool man was very angry. He had no idea why his children had not been accepted. The manager that came with him enrolled his children after James and was immediately accepted without any problem. The following week, James had asked to speak to the headmaster, but he was perpetually unavailable. He was so shocked.

    Rumor started circulating about the rejection, leaked from a board member's daughter and Thomas caught wind of it at the golf club. Thomas had made friends with old Mr. Kim and welcomed James to the community with open arms. James had confided in him about all of this. It just broke my heart when I heard that from Thomas. The board at Stormy Preparatory School was notorious for only allowing white children in, the remnants of a long line of people who couldn't let the past go. Thomas had spoken to James about the rumors and assured him they were more than rumors. His dad's business had floated the town, employing thousands of people through the years and this was the gratitude they had? It wasn't a difficult decision for James to relocate the plant to another community, one more caring and accepting of him and his family. He closed the plant and moved. I remember how sad Thomas was to see him go and the embarrassment that he felt for the poorly executed, ignorant decisions reflective of an era that should have never been. James kept in touch with Thomas until his passing.

Such a sad story with the closing of the plant. Stormy took an economic plunge. It never really recovered until all of the litigation started drawing attention and people to Stormy. Where we used to have an honorable company keeping our families afloat, we now have such shameful fanfare. Oh, honey look what time it is! You need to get on the road. We will have time for more history later. I've got plenty of cards to go through with you. Get on the road now. Be careful!" Miss Nella shooed me away playfully.

"Yes, mam! Thank you, Miss Nella. I appreciate your filling me in. What a shame! I'm embarrassed to have gone to school there. Honestly, I had no idea how bad it was. I certainly wasn't raised to be that way. I'll be careful. I should be back before four o'clock. I promised Nola Mae I would visit her parents' graves with her today."

Chapter 22

I wouldn't say I was a Pollyanna, but my glasses have always been a little tinted rose colored. I try to see the best in people, but unfortunately, I have met too many people that don't. Talking to Miss Nella about Mr. Kim and enrolling his children at Stormy Preparatory School and then being rejected, fueled a whole lot of memories to fill my drive to Mobile.

So many fun memories were conjured up as I thought about the years I had attended Stormy Preparatory School. There were good people there too, many good people. Because we were not a wealthy family, I wasn't sure how I was accepted. I wanted to play sports even from a young age. I had always been to public school in my elementary years, prior to attending there. And we had looked at the public-school sports programs, but there were too many people wanting to play and too few slots open. So even though there would be tuition, my mom wanted me to get to do something I wanted to, so badly. So we tried it. I had built some strong relationships there and I wanted to stay there from junior high on throughout high school.

My mind started racing as I thought about my volleyball coach. He was our headmaster too. From the start I knew he didn't like me, and it always made things awkward. But it made me work harder, not to impress him, but to reach goals for myself with or without his support. I'm sure money had a lot to do with his not liking me. I kind of chuckled out loud when I thought about an incident where he called me out of class my senior year. I didn't ever cause any problems, so I wasn't really worried. He asked me to sit down. He told me I had made volleyball State All Stars. I was ecstatic at the thought of missing school all week to get to play volleyball. Then he told me he didn't vote for me, but every other coach in the region did. Who tells somebody that, especially a child? At that point I think he thought he would hurt my feelings, but in reality it just made him look bad. What a jerk! Then I laughed. I'm glad I made it on merit, not his good graces. All of these memories had me a bit distracted. I'm not sure how long a red truck had been following me, but I turned off the Bay Minette exit and went into the gas station there. I told the attendant I thought I was being followed. She said "Hold on sugar, my husband is a deputy. I'm going to see if he will come by and do a check. You stay right here with me." It didn't take much convincing. I grabbed a couple of snacks and drinks and waited a couple of minutes.

Mr. Blankenship, in the meantime, had pulled up to the gas station and was waiting for me to come out. The deputy pulled up, and already having been alerted to the situation blocked Mr. Blankenship in. The cashier and I walked outside and stood by the door, listening in. We knew we were safe with the deputy there. The deputy proceeded to ask what business Mr. Blankenship had this morning at the gas station. Mr. Blankenship told him he was just taking a break from driving to Mobile. Boy was he angry, face red and almost shouting at the deputy. "Sir if you are just taking a break, why are you so angry?" "I'm not angry!" he shouted at the deputy. "Okay sir, well then you need to be either getting gas or getting on your way. Mr. Blankenship turned around. The deputy got in his car to free Mr. Blankenship up to make his decision. On his way it was. He turned back towards Stormy.

"Do you know that man ma'am?" he asked me. "I know who he is, and I know he doesn't like me for some reason." "Ma'am you're not from around here? Your tags say Missouri." "No sir, I haven't lived here for a long time. I'm working on my mama and daddy's house up in Stormy. I was just headed to Mobile to get some supplies. I didn't even notice that he was behind me until a few miles ago. He must have been hanging back. I'm a little nervous to head on to Mobile," I said to the deputy. "You go ahead. I got his license plate number and vehicle description. I'll wait right up here at the exit for a bit and then pass this information on down the road." He said very protective of me. "Thank you so much sir, I really appreciate it." And he nodded his head.

I turned on the 80s station and let my mind wander again to the good times and good people I knew in Stormy. That lasted all the way to Mobile.

White knuckle driving home later that day wore me out. I didn't even feel like going anywhere else but where I needed to in Mobile. Every red truck or honestly red car caused me to do a double take and increased my anxiety tremendously. I was home by 1:30. Maisy had gone with me, and all this wore her out too. We were both ready for a nap. I had promised I would go on a walk with Nola

Mae later today, but I needed to rest first. She wanted me to visit her mama and daddy's graves and take them some flowers.

Maisy and I napped for a bit and then I went over about four to help her pick flowers. We picked several kinds of flowers. There was a beautiful patch of baby's breath on Mr. Blankenship side of the yard that spilled over into Nola Mae's. His truck wasn't home so I was about to snap a bunch with my garden shears and Nola Mae yells "STOP!" I screamed, thinking it was a snake or something and scrambled away from the area. "What in the world, Nola Mae? What is wrong?" She started whimpering and wouldn't speak, couldn't speak.

"Nola Mae, I know something's wrong." We slowly sat down on the grass. "I know something traumatic happened to you when you were about ten years old. She looked up at me with really scared, tear filled eyes. "You know?" she said shaking. "You know about Susan?" she asked. She was starting to open up. All of a sudden, Mr. Blankenship appeared in his backyard. "Leave her alone, she is crazy. Don't say I didn't warn you!" he yelled through clenched teeth. She shrunk into a ball on the grass. "Good grief, Mr.

Blankenship. Why do you have to say that? We were just picking flowers for her parents' graves." I tried to stay cool like I would with any angry parent at school, but my anger got the best of me. I told him he needed to leave her alone and to leave me alone as well. He stomped off. No doubt planning his next terror attack on me.

I got Nola Mae inside and told her to lock her doors. I worried about her safety. She asked me again if I knew about Susan and I told her I didn't but would love to know more. She showed me a poem she had written when she was ten years old and told me to keep it safe. I folded it up and put it in my pocket. I had to some way keep Nola Mae safe until I could get more things sorted out.

"Do not let anyone in your house no matter what, do you hear me Nola Mae? I'm going to try to get you some help today. I don't think you're safe here. Now go pack your bag like you were going to stay somewhere for a week. I'll be back very soon.

Nola Mae agreed to everything and ran back to her room to pack. Mama had several friends that worked with the mental health program in the area and I called one of them that I knew worked the tri-county region. I talked over with her about sending Nola Mae to a facility until I could get some answers. She agreed to come with me to her house and transport her to a facility outside of Stormy.

When I got back to Nola Mae's house I headed to the back yard hoping I wouldn't see her out and about. As I approached the back door, the window to the back door had been busted in. I panicked and started yelling for Nola Mae. Thankfully I could hear her whimpering. "Nola Mae, can you let me in the front door?" I saw her body move and then saw her get to her feet, still whimpering. I ran back around front, and she opened the door for me. Mrs. Jenkins was there by that time. Nola Mae buried her head in my shoulder crying and shaking uncontrollably. "Mrs. Jenkins is here to take you on a trip. She was a friend of my mama's and you can trust her."

Just then Mr. Blankenship came out onto his porch. Nola Mae's knees gave out and she fell to the floor and curled up in a ball again. I turned to Mrs. Jenkins. "Tell me that's not a trauma response, Mrs. Jenkins" I said disgusted. "Yes ma'am. It is." Mr. Blankenship yelled "I have warned you enough, leave her alone, she's crazy." "Mr. Blankenship your warning was heeded. Nola Mae is experiencing some episodes of "craziness" as you say and we are getting her help. You needn't worry about her anymore. She is getting the help she has needed for a long time." I said very confidently. With this news, he went back inside and slammed his front door so hard the glass window broke. "Serves him right!" I said louder than I thought. "Let's get her in your car quickly." I told Mrs. Jenkins. I told Nola Mae he was gone, and she needed to get to her feet. She complied weakly and Mrs. Jenkins grabbed her suitcase. "Lola Mae where are your house keys? I'm going to hold on to them, while you're gone and get your window fixed." She pointed to a set of keys hanging on the wall. "Okay, let's go. You're going to be very safe. I will come see you tomorrow. Thank you, Mrs. Jenkins, you're truly a lifesaver." I closed the door on Nola Mae's side and got in my car hoping this was the end of the drama for the day.

Exhausted from everything, I went back home and settled in on the couch, grabbed my notebook and my phone and started my search. Who was Susan? What did babies' breath have to do with the trauma? And how does Mr. Blankenship fit into the trauma? How am I supposed to fit all this together? I shifted positions on the sofa and it made me remember I had folded up that poem that Nola Mae wrote when she was just ten years old and tucked it into my back pocket. I slowly unfolded it, looked at the rudimentary handwriting and followed the lines written just like a ten-year-old would write.

    Playing jacks one night

    between the spindles I got a fright

    a man with a shovel, a girl he hit

    on the back of the head when he was pitching a fit

    she went down to the ground, and I thought maybe

    he was mad at her because she said she was having a baby

    he buried her there in the flower bed

    and babies' breath blooms on top of her head.

Oh my gosh! Oh, my heart is broken. "She witnessed a murder!" I said this out loud and now I wish I hadn't. I hope Mr. Blankenship was nowhere around listening.

My thoughts wandered back to the poem. Mr. Blankenship was the man that killed Susan, but Susan who? I wish Miss Nella was up still. It was only ten o'clock. I looked out the kitchen window and her bedroom light was still on. I reached for my phone to call her and my front porch light sensor came on. I looked at the camera app on my phone and it was Mr. Blankenship. He had some kind of nerve showing up at my house this late. I called 911 instead of Miss Nella and asked for someone to come to the house. A police car came promptly with lights on. Mr. Blankenship didn't make it too far in the yard before he took a tumble on one of those rogue wisteria vines I had neglected to cut. The police officer picked him up and asked him what he was doing at my house at 10:00 at night. He told them he was worried about Nola Mae and thought I could tell him where she was. When I heard him say that I choked. "No way!" I said demonstratively. The officer asked why he ran and he said he didn't want people to think he was having an affair. I couldn't help but respond to this with a very loud "WHAT?" I'm sure with the most disgusted look on my face. The amused officer seemed to also think this was not credible. Mr. Blankenship is an excellent liar, years of practice I'm sure. The police officer got him completely on his feet and told him to get home. Mr. Blankenship walked a few blocks to the Presbyterian Church and got in his truck to drive home. I asked the officer to stay for a minute. I went over all the places that Mr. Blankenship had shown up, including the exit at Bay Minette. I'm not writing a formal complaint about all of this yet, but it is unnerving.

By this time Miss Nella had come over and told me to come spend the night with her. I asked the officer to stay while I packed a few things, including the poem from Nola Mae. I couldn't believe how much I knew and now I needed to prove it all. I harnessed Maisy and headed over to Miss Nella's with her. Settling in, I sent a text to Mrs. Jenkins about details of this facility. I planned on leaving early in the morning, to pick up donuts and fresh flowers out of her yard to take with me. I asked for a police officer to meet me at eight o'clock at Nola Mae's and wait nearby while I did this.

About 9:00 am I arrived at the facility. They had taken Nola Mae to a room where she was held in a high security unit, under protective custody. I signed in to go talk to her. She was beaming when I came in and quickly moved across the room to hug me. I showed her the donuts and she said "Yummy!" and then she saw the flowers I picked and shouted "NO! Those are for the baby!" "Nola Mae, it's okay. I know about the baby. I read about it in your poem." I said gently. "You did?" "Yes, I did. But I still don't know who Susan is. Can you tell me? You are safe now and no one can hurt you, I promise." "Really Cacky? No one will hurt me for telling?" "No one, Nola Mae. No one is ever going to hurt you for telling and you are going to get the help you need." "Okay," she began. Holding back tears while she told her story was one of the hardest things I've ever done. Her psychiatrist and a police officer were present. I turned on my phone recorder while the others took notes and now we could see where we would go from there.

Meanwhile orders were being written to exhume the body of Susan and her baby. After visiting with Nola Mae a bit, I needed to head back home. I needed to be there when they exhumed the bodies.

I asked them to take care not to destroy the flowers. I wanted to take two bunches to put on Susan's parents' graves. It was the least I could do.

An angry, far past angry Mr. Blankenship threw the court orders down and pitched another fit, possibly similar to the one he pitched that night. Strange how things come full circle.

I wept as her body was retrieved gently from the grave. Nestled within her bones was the bones of the baby. They lay right there where they should have been, close to their mama. With the bodies as evidence to corroborate Nola Mae's story, Mr. Blankenship was handcuffed and read his rights as they lowered his head to put him in the back of the police car. Three lives were taken away because of his selfish actions; Susan, her baby and Nola Mae. But thankfully Nola Mae can recover some and live a fairly normal life without Mr. Blankenship living next door.

Just as I asked, they took care to save the flowers. I gathered two bunches and walked down to the cemetery to put them on Susan's parents' graves, grieving the lives that have been taken away. I told them I was sorry for their loss, but now everyone could rest in peace.

Chapter 23

Thankful that I had recorded Nola Mae's story, I was able to play it back and write it down. She was such a great storyteller and I'm thankful that it is now on paper instead of held captive in her mind. Here it is.

"Well, you know that slamming screen doors always happens in the summertime in Stormy. But y'all know there are two kinds though, right? One caused by a spring on the door and the other by someone pushing it hard, real hard. The first one usually meant us kids running in and out of the house and it usually ended up with Mama fussing and telling us to stop slamming doors. The other slam usually meant someone was angry or being a sassy mouth.

One night I heard the second one happen. I had been playing jacks on the front porch. This was the most horrible night I could ever think of and the night that changed my life. I was really good at jacks. I could play with my eyes closed. So, I was able to play under the dim porch light that had moths and bugs flying all around it.

The screen door that slammed this night was caused by somebody being mad with somebody else. It wasn't my screen door, but it was the Smithson's door. They lived one house down. They were yelling something awful, and it made me kind of scared. I stopped playing jacks for a minute because I didn't want them to see me there. I got scared enough with all the yelling that I made my way to the corner of the porch and hid in the dark. I tightened my hold around my knees and listened in. "Susan, you have to go to Margie's house, you are starting to show. I won't have our name ruined because you decided to do things you shouldn't. I didn't raise you like that!" Mrs. Smithson was shouting at Susan. I have heard her say that in my head for many years. "Mama I wouldn't go stay with Aunt Marge for nothing. You can't and won't make me. Don't look for me Mama, I won't be back. Tell daddy I love him, but I have obviously brought a shame that you can't forgive. I love you too, Mama." The rest of this conversation was burned in my brain, too. I didn't know what it all meant. I just remember it.

And then the screen door slammed so loud. I watched Susan stomp down the porch steps and head down the sidewalk with a suitcase and her purse in her hand. Susan looked around. She didn't see anyone looking. Then she sneaked into the side yard between my house and the mean neighbor's house. There were no outside lights around the house except a thin line of light coming through the closed curtains of Mr. Blankenship's study. I knew that room well from when I went over to play there when I was little. That room was off limits to us kids.

I was trying to hold my breath so no one would hear me, but I saw Susan rap quietly on the windowpane to his study, I gasped. I don't think she heard me. The first rap wasn't enough, and I heard Susan say whispering "For Pete's sake where is he?" The second rap was successful, and a surprised and angry Mr. Blankenship drew back the curtains. He pointed to the backyard. He was angry as a hornet. Susan quietly agreed and headed that direction directly behind the garage.

The moonlight behind the garage allowed me to see the two figures standing there. He grabbed her by the arm and told her no one better ever find out that this baby was his. Susan's chest got big like she was holding her breath. She got away from him and said something about he made a promise to her. She turned around to stomp off and he grabbed her again. I was sitting there shaking and it was hard to breathe. And then it happened. I saw Mr. Blankenship lift his shovel and hit Susan hard on the back of the head. She fell down and it didn't look like she was alive. She wasn't breathing at all. I kept watching for her to move. I half screamed and nearly passed out when I realized she was really dead. I was frozen! Mr. Blankenship heard me and turned and walked my way very quickly. He was moving too fast in my direction I couldn't feel my body or move it to get up and run. But I could feel tears rolling down my cheek.

Mr. Blankenship came to the edge of the porch putting his scary face between the spindles and said "You ever speak a word of this and not only will I do the same to you but everyone in your family." Oh, I was so scared. I didn't want anyone else to get hit with a shovel or killed by Mr. Blankenship. He turned back around and marched back over to where Susan was lying. I still couldn't move and had to sit there and watch him dig a hole and bury Susan in that hole, I couldn't stop staring. I tried. He then took her suitcase and purse and put them in his burn barrel and lit it on fire. I watched it burn until I fell asleep.

The next thing I knew I was being picked up by strong muscular hands. I let out a scream until under the porch light I could see it was my Daddy's sweet face. I began to cry and reached my arms around my daddy's neck until he laid me down on the bed to sleep for the night. That was the first night of the nightmares that I still have every single night.

Susan's Mama sat on the porch every night waiting and watching for Susan to return. She would check the mailbox several times a day, each time crying. I thought maybe she was waiting on a letter from Susan. Every time I would see her go to the mailbox, my stomach would hurt. I wanted to tell her, but I couldn't. I knew Mr. Blankenship would kill us all. Mrs. Smithson never knew that Susan never really left at all and Mr. Blankenship made sure that it was never told. I wish I could see Mrs. Smithson now and tell her, but I know she already knows. Maybe she has even gotten to see Susan again in Heaven. I sure hope so."

Chapter 24

Now that Nola Mae has told her story, and Mr. Blankenship arrested and charged in Susan's and the baby's murder, I feel like I can concentrate on Mama and Daddy's house and get it on the market.

Being here only a few weeks has felt like months. I have learned so much in such a short period of time, possibly more than I learned in an entire year of college.

There is still so much to do here, and my summer always goes too fast. This morning, I am making my list of things left to do. The doorbell rings. I immediately am startled, stunned and can't move. Then I let out a heavy relieving sigh and get up to answer the door, realizing Mr. Blankenship is behind bars now.

Walking to the front door, I can see the silhouettes of multiple people. "What in the world?" I say out loud, almost to the door.

Upon opening the door, a whole crew of people, dressed in old work clothes, parade into my house uninvited, but not unwelcomed. The porch chat ladies came to help, every one of them.

"We are here to ease your burden, put us to work!" Miss Nella said. "Yes," the rest agreed. And so, one woman's work was spread among me and six highly capable, skilled ladies that I had grown to know and love since I had been here. My original goal was to just come, get my Mama and Daddy's house ready to sell and head back to Kansas City. I had no idea the trip that was going to change my life. I sure was going to miss these ladies.

Mama and Daddy's house was more than ready to be listed. With five hours of work with seven people, it looked good. I will be forever grateful for my porch chat friends.

Miss Nella invited us all back over to her house for an early dinner. We laughed and ate and enjoyed one last porch chat before I headed home. It was just what I needed! I hugged each one as they left and thanked them for helping me out. What a tremendous blessing they had all been.

And now for my last visit with Miss Nella before I left. I was snuggling up on the porch swing when she got up to go retrieve her recipe box from the kitchen. Upon her return to the porch, she scooted next to me on the swing. She had never done that before. It made me catch my breath, so I didn't start crying.

Miss Nella opens the box. She starts to speak, hesitates and then continues. "Cacky, you are such a talented writer. I knew you would become a writer since you were a girl, from making my grocery lists for me when you were younger to writing stories as a teenager. You always had a notebook handy.

When your brother was killed, you became head of the household. You had to. I think your mama started changing from grief. It really took a toll on her. With your dad gone most of the time, which really was a blessing, I know the burden went on you. You shouldered so much at such a young age. I saw your notebook go away and traded in for a checkbook, "how to" books and then college books. I'm thankful that you picked up your notebook again. When I saw that you had published a book, it made me so happy and thankful.

"Miss Nella, you really ought to write a book with all those stories tucked away in this recipe box." I reached over and gently took the box from Miss Nella and started flipping through the cards. One after the other, these cards told decades of stories with incredibly detailed information on each card.

"No mam," Miss Nella said. "That's your job. This box has been waiting years for you to come get it and take it home." I drew back and looked at Miss Nella in shock and disbelief. "Really, Miss Nella? You have spent a lifetime gathering this information." "Only your lifetime, child. I did this for you and now it's time to put it all to use. Write this story, for both of us and for your mama." Miss Nella said through tears. "Oh, you bet I will Miss Nella! This means the world to me! I will make you proud," I said grabbing Miss Nella's hand and squeezing it tight. "You always have, Cacky, you always have. And your mama was certainly proud of you too! Don't you ever forget that!" "I won't Miss Nella. Miss Nella? I love you." "I love you too, Cacky."

This book is a work of fiction. Any of the characters, places, names, or incidents are the product of the author's imagination. Any resemblance to people, places, occurrences or incidents are purely fictitious and/or coincidental.

Made in the USA
Monee, IL
15 June 2024